P9-ECL-251

Still can't get enough cowboys?

Popular Harlequin Blaze author Debbie Rawlins
keeps readers in the saddle
with her continuing miniseries,

Made in Montana.

Since the McAllisters opened a dude ranch catering to single women, the sleepy town of Blackfoot Falls has become a lot more interesting....

Get your hands on a hot cowboy with

#701 Barefoot Blue Jean Night
(August 2012)

#713 Own the Night
(October 2012)

#725 On a Snowy Christmas Night
(December 2012)

#737 You're Still the One
(February 2013)

#744 No One Needs to Know
(April 2013)

#753 From This Moment On
(May 2013)

And remember, the sexiest cowboys are Made in Montana!

Dear Reader,

We have exciting news! Starting in January, the Harlequin Blaze books you know and love will be getting a brand-new look. And it's *hot!* Turn to the back of this book for a sneak peek....

But don't worry—nothing else about the Blaze books has changed. You'll still find those unforgettable love stories with intrepid heroines, hot, hunky heroes and a double dose of sizzle!

So be sure to check out our new supersexy covers. You'll find these newly packaged Blaze editions on the shelves December 18th, 2012, wherever you buy your books.

In the meantime, check out this month's red-hot reads.

LET IT SNOW by Leslie Kelly and Jennifer LaBrecque
(A Blazing Bedtime Stories Holiday Edition)

HIS FIRST NOELLE by Rhonda Nelson
(Men Out of Uniform)

ON A SNOWY CHRISTMAS NIGHT by Debbi Rawlins
(Made in Montana)

NICE & NAUGHTY by Tawny Weber

ALL I WANT FOR CHRISTMAS
by Lori Wilde, Kathleen O'Reilly and Candace Havens
(A Sizzling Yuletide Anthology)

HERS FOR THE HOLIDAYS by Samantha Hunter
(The Berringers)

Happy holidays!

Brenda Chin
Senior Editor
Harlequin Blaze

Debbi Rawlins

ON A SNOWY CHRISTMAS NIGHT

If you purchased this book without a cover you should be aware that this book is stolen property. It was reported as "unsold and destroyed" to the publisher, and neither the author nor the publisher has received any payment for this "stripped book."

Recycling programs
for this product may
not exist in your area.

ISBN-13: 978-0-373-79729-5

ON A SNOWY CHRISTMAS NIGHT

Copyright © 2012 by Debbi Quattrone

All rights reserved. Except for use in any review, the reproduction or utilization of this work in whole or in part in any form by any electronic, mechanical or other means, now known or hereafter invented, including xerography, photocopying and recording, or in any information storage or retrieval system, is forbidden without the written permission of the publisher, Harlequin Enterprises Limited, 225 Duncan Mill Road, Don Mills, Ontario, Canada M3B 3K9.

This is a work of fiction. Names, characters, places and incidents are either the product of the author's imagination or are used fictitiously, and any resemblance to actual persons, living or dead, business establishments, events or locales is entirely coincidental.

This edition published by arrangement with Harlequin Books S.A.

For questions and comments about the quality of this book, please contact us at CustomerService@Harlequin.com.

® and TM are trademarks of Harlequin Enterprises Limited or its corporate affiliates. Trademarks indicated with ® are registered in the United States Patent and Trademark Office, the Canadian Trade Marks Office and in other countries.

www.Harlequin.com

Printed in U.S.A.

ABOUT THE AUTHOR

Debbi Rawlins lives in central Utah, out in the country, surrounded by woods and deer and wild turkeys. It's quite a change for a city girl who didn't even know where the state of Utah was until a few years ago. Of course, unfamiliarity has never stopped her. Between her junior and senior years of college, she spontaneously left her home in Hawaii and bummed around Europe for five weeks by herself. And much to her parents' delight, returned home with only a quarter in her wallet.

Books by Debbi Rawlins

HARLEQUIN BLAZE

13—IN HIS WILDEST DREAMS
36—EDUCATING GINA
60—HANDS ON
112—ANYTHING GOES...
143—HE'S ALL THAT*
159—GOOD TO BE BAD
183—A GLIMPSE OF FIRE
220—HOT SPOT**
250—THE HONEYMOON THAT WASN'T
312—SLOW HAND LUKE
351—IF HE ONLY KNEW...*
368—WHAT SHE *REALLY* WANTS FOR CHRISTMAS†
417—ALL OR NOTHING
455—ONCE AN OUTLAW††
467—ONCE A REBEL††
491—TEXAS HEAT
509—TEXAS BLAZE
528—LONE STAR LOVER††
603—SECOND TIME LUCKY‡
609—DELICIOUS DO-OVER‡
632—EXTRA INNINGS
701—BAREFOOT BLUE JEAN NIGHT§
713—OWN THE NIGHT§

*Men To Do
**Do Not Disturb
†Million Dollar Secrets
††Stolen from Time
‡Spring Break
§Made in Montana

1

THE BRISK DECEMBER air smelled like snow. None was forecasted for the next few days, but when it started getting dark this time of year, the Montana temperature invariably dropped.

Jesse McAllister pulled up the collar of his leather bomber jacket, hunched his shoulders against the cold and finished fueling his truck. This week he was using Leo's gas station, which was situated at the edge of town. Next time he'd fill up at Earl's, Blackfoot Falls's only other station, five blocks north on the other end of Main Street. Jesse had gone to school with both men's sons so he was careful to spread the business.

The multicolored Christmas lights twisting around the flagpole and arching over the tiny town square blinked on just as Jesse climbed behind the wheel. He smiled when the giant elm tree lit up and knew that it was Miriam Lemmon who'd flipped the switch. Tomorrow evening it would be Mabel's turn. The elderly twins had been in charge of seasonal decorations since before Jesse was born.

The familiarity should have been comforting. But in the year and a half since he'd returned home, there'd been no solace. His family's fourth-generation ranch was struggling. It didn't matter that the poor economy was affecting everyone.

Hell, he'd crossed an ocean to fight for his country, learned how to fly everything from large planes to small helicopters, and yet there wasn't a damn thing he could do to pull the ranch out of the red.

He'd been eager to come home after his air-force duty, but since then it seemed he'd been nothing but dead weight. Sucking in oxygen yet contributing nothing.

Winter made everything worse. During the spring and summer months, with the calving and roundups and irrigation constantly going haywire, there didn't seem to be enough hours in the day. But since the final cut of hay, work was sparse and they had a bunkhouse full of hands who needed steady paychecks. Like Cole and Trace, Jesse still pitched in, made himself useful the best way he knew how. But his brothers, they belonged here, not him.

Not feeling like heading back to the Sundance just yet, he decided to cruise down Main Street to see if Noah was in his office. Even three blocks away, Jesse could see the sheriff's truck parked at the curb. That didn't necessarily mean anything. Noah could've walked home or over to Marge's diner for supper.

Jesse drove past the Cut and Curl, where his mother always got her hair done, past the hardware store, Ernie's barber shop and the fabric store. He slowed to a crawl when he got to the second residential side street and peered at the third house down. No lights on, so Noah wasn't home. The county provided the small two-bedroom house for him as part of the sheriff's compensation. But mostly he spent his free time out at the Sundance, just as he had when they were teenagers.

Noah had always been part of the family, and sometimes it was easier for Jesse to talk to him rather than Cole. Even though Jesse was only a year younger, his brother had been the one to fill their father's shoes when he'd died of cancer while Jesse was still in college. It was a McAllister tradition—the reins were handed to the oldest son…as they should be.

Jesse drove past the Watering Hole, where the usual Friday-evening crowd hung out after they'd cashed their checks. Then he saw Noah through the open blinds of the sheriff's office. Roy, one of the deputies, was on his way out the door, so Jesse parked his truck at the curb.

By the time he went inside, Noah was standing at the window, looking out and frowning. "Where's your Jeep?"

"Traded it in." Jesse went straight to the half-filled coffeepot. The brew was dark, which meant Noah had made it. Reminded Jesse of some of the joe he'd stomached in Afghanistan. So strong you could use it for diesel. "This stuff fresh?"

Noah nodded. "Why did you do that? You loved that Jeep."

Jesse hunted in the upper oak cabinet for a clean mug, found one and sniffed it for good measure. "It wasn't practical."

"Yeah, because you guys don't have enough pickups at the Sundance."

Jesse shrugged. "I got a good deal on the Dodge," he said. "It's secondhand but has only forty-two thousand miles."

Noah eyed him thoughtfully, likely wondering what had brought on Jesse's change of heart. He'd wanted a Jeep since before he'd learned to drive. The first thing he'd done after returning from Afghanistan was find a dealership and drive the latest model off the lot. It wasn't until later, when he'd seen the disrepair of the ranch, that he'd realized what a selfish bastard he'd been.

But that probably wasn't the only thing Noah was wondering about. Jesse wasn't himself and everyone, including Noah, thought the war had changed him. Jesse knew the war had nothing to do with his restlessness.

Sure, he'd seen things no human being should have to witness. War was never pretty. And yeah, even though he'd been a tanker pilot and not one of the fighter jocks, he'd flown some damn hairy missions, but he hadn't experienced anything like the men with boots on the ground. As far as deployments went, he'd had it fairly easy.

No, his problem was pretty basic. After living in Montana most of his life, being completely sure that his duty and his destiny were bound up in the Sundance, he didn't belong here anymore. Ironic that it had about killed him to give the military all those years in exchange for teaching him how to fly. He'd even chosen a college close enough that he could come home most weekends. And now…each day his sense of belonging seemed to fade even more.

"Weren't you supposed to fly to Billings to pick up a pair of pit bulls?" Noah finally said, while he topped up his coffee.

"The neighbor of the woman who runs the center there adopted them."

"That was lucky."

"Yeah, people are too biased against pit bulls. They're good dogs as long as they're raised right." Jesse sipped his coffee and stared idly out the window, suddenly feeling foolish that he'd stopped by. It wasn't as if he needed advice. He knew what he had to do. Volunteering for animal search-and-rescue had taken the edge off his discontent but it wasn't helping his family.

"Sit down." Noah indicated the sorry black vinyl-and-chrome chair, then sat behind his desk. "What are you doing in town, anyway?"

"I had to pick up some fencing wire and fuel the truck."

"It's quiet around here without Sundance guests coming and going. Rachel take any reservations for January?"

Jesse sighed. The family had agreed they'd close the dude ranch for the holidays, but his sister was a pushover. "She's got a woman coming in next weekend."

"A week before Christmas?" Noah frowned over the rim

of his mug. "I thought she'd shut down for the month of December."

"She's making an exception. The woman is volunteering over at Safe Haven and was desperate for a place to stay." Jesse shrugged. "You know Rachel. Couldn't say no. You still going to New York to see Alana?"

Noah grinned like a ten-year-old with a new puppy. "I leave next Thursday. My sisters are coming with their families to spend Christmas with the folks."

Jesse managed a smile. Not that he wasn't happy for his friend. It was the holidays he was dreading. He hadn't heard anything about the annual open house his mother usually hosted, but he knew it had to be on the calendar. Even if they did have to shell out a few bucks for the food and beer, no one would deny her the McAllister tradition.

"Which airport you flying out of?" Jesse asked.

"Billings. Anything closer was either booked or involved too many layovers."

"Need a ride?"

Noah's brows furrowed with curiosity. "I thought you'd be looking forward to spending the time with the family. This is what...only the second holiday you've been home?"

"Jesus, it's just a ride."

Noah leaned back, a self-deprecating smile pulling at his mouth. "Thanks, I'm taking my truck." He took another sip, his probing eyes staying on Jesse. "How've you been, buddy?"

"You know..." He shrugged. "Good. I've been doing a lot of flying for different shelters." Nothing new, and not what his friend was asking. Jesse let out a gushing breath. "I'm thinking about reenlisting."

Noah's mouth opened, and he quickly set down his mug. "You gotta be kidding. Shit," he said when he clearly realized that Jesse was dead serious. "What do Cole and the rest of the family say about it?"

"They don't know." Jesse looked him square in the eye. "This stays between you and me."

"Why reenlist?" Noah shook his head. "You hated being away from Montana."

"I'm no good here. At least with an officer's salary I can send home money, plus the bonus I'll get for committing to another ten years."

Noah frowned, looking so troubled Jesse was sorry as hell he'd opened his mouth. "You talked to someone from the air force about this already?"

"Just enough to know what's what."

"Big mistake, buddy. Especially if it's just about the money. You'll break your mother's heart."

Jesse stared into his cold coffee. "Yeah, well, I gotta do what's best for everyone."

Noah muttered a curse. "If you think tearing yourself away from the ranch and your family to make a buck is the right thing, you've got a hell of a lot more thinking to do."

Wasn't that the problem? The more thinking Jesse did, the more lost he felt.

SHEA MONROE STARED out the large plate-glass window of her San Jose office, the phone pressed to her ear as she listened to her mother complain about her new stepchildren. The older one had dared to move the silk poinsettia topiary an inch out of place. The other two…well, their existence alone was enough to make her mom complain.

Age was supposed to mellow a person, or so Shea had heard. In her mother's case the new wrinkles, which had to be instantly treated with BOTOX, or the occasional sprout of gray hair only made her crankier. Oh, Shea loved her. Didn't mean she wanted to listen to her rant.

"Mom?" This was the third time Shea had tried to get a word in.

"If I'd been smart, I would've refused to decorate for Christmas. Let Richard have his office party at the Four Seasons. He's there half the time, anyway, entertaining one client or another—"

A designer had done all the work. For that matter, a nanny watched Richard's children, and a housekeeper kept their minimansion spotless. Women as beautiful and clever as Leticia Kelly didn't…

No, that wasn't right. Shea rubbed her temple. It wasn't Kelly anymore. Was it Griffin? Yeah, maybe Griffin. For having a high IQ, Shea sure had a lousy memory for names. But then, if her parents would stay off the marriage carousel, she might be able to hang on to a name for more than five minutes.

Finally, there was a tiny break in the monologue and Shea jumped in before she missed her chance. "I'm not coming for Christmas."

"What?" A brief pause, and then her mother said, "Don't think you're going to your father's house. You can't. That wasn't the deal."

"What deal?"

"He had you for Thanksgiving. I get you for Christmas."

"Mom, I'm twenty-seven, not twelve. You two don't get to decide where I spend the holidays anymore."

"But you promised."

"Uh, no, actually, I didn't."

"My God, Shea, you can't abandon me to these people."

"You mean your family?" She smiled sadly. It would've been nice if her mother had said that Christmas wouldn't be the same without her, or even that she'd be missed. "Look, I'm not going to spend the holidays with Dad, either."

"Please don't tell me you're back together with that Brian idiot."

"No." She glanced toward her open door. It was after six.

Brian would have left already, along with the new love of his life, Serena from accounting. "You know better."

Or did she? Unlike Shea, her mother couldn't abide living alone. She'd been a nineteen-year-old cocktail waitress when she'd met Shea's father at the hotel where he'd been attending a conference. Within eleven months they'd married and had Shea. It took them ten years to divorce, which was a miracle. No two people were less suited for each other. Her father was a prominent theoretical physicist, and her mother… well, while she wasn't necessarily bright, she was clever and a stunner with an eye for fashion. Had a knack for snagging rich men, too, considering her roots were crusty blue collar. The longest she'd been between husbands was about a year.

Shea had hated the between times. Moving from town to town, school to school and finally to boarding school. And getting used to new "fathers." She hated change of any kind, even if it meant staying in a relationship that had run its course. Give her a steady routine any day—she liked having things she could count on. It had been Brian who'd left her. Nearly three years they'd been together, had shared an apartment for almost two of them. She supposed she should feel something—sadness, regret, maybe even anger over the callous way he'd broken up with her a year ago. She felt nothing.

No, that wasn't entirely true, she thought, with a satisfied smile aimed at the prized view of the skyline outside her window. She was pretty pleased to have the corner office Brian coveted. Hardly a charitable thought, but too bad. She hadn't asked for the prime spot. In fact, it was a waste. Her gaze was usually glued to her computer monitor. Not that she minded. She liked the total focus necessary in her job as a computer software engineer for a high-tech corporation. Her boss had only given the office to her to emphasize her importance to the company. They were always giving her perks and bonuses.

That was part of the reason Brian had called it quits. She'd outpaced him and grown too successful. And her terrible social skills were also a factor. Being rushed through school had its price. She'd had only one friend and two dates by the time she graduated high school at fifteen. College had been more of the same.

But she was getting better. Every day. Though only when she paid attention and put herself out there, going to a movie or having a drink with a coworker instead of locking herself away with her computer and iPad. That's why it was important to put her foot down and not let her mother steamroll her into coming for Christmas.

"Are you still there?"

"What?" Hearing her mother's impatient sigh, Shea realized she'd zoned out. "I have to get back to work, but I wanted to let you know about Christmas."

"Wait a minute. Don't you dare hang up. Nothing is settled."

"Yes, it is. I've already booked a flight."

"For where?"

"Montana."

"What the hell's in Montana?"

Shea smiled. Her mother wore Prada these days but her vernacular hadn't changed. "I'm going to be doing volunteer work."

"For God's sake, Shea, we've got homeless people here in Phoenix. Can't you sling hash at a shelter here?"

Jeez. "I'm not going to be serving at a soup kitchen. It's an animal shelter."

"Well, I'm sure they have places like that around here. There certainly are enough mangy-looking dogs prowling the neighborhood and knocking over garbage cans. You can still change your airline ticket."

"I could," Shea agreed calmly, although her annoyance was climbing. "But I'm not going to. I want to do this."

"It's Christmas. You're supposed to be with family."

"Don't take this personally, Mom. This has nothing to do with you." Shea didn't know why she bothered. Of course her mother took it personally. Everything was about her. "The place where I'll be volunteering specializes in large animals. Like horses...you know how much I've wanted—"

"Damn right I'm taking it personally," she said, cutting Shea off. "You spent Thanksgiving with your father and that squawking brood of his, but you won't come to see me?"

She would not give in. Nope. Not this time. She stared at her hand, surprised that she'd started drumming her fingers on the desk. What usually came next was counting in multiples of three with each tap of her finger.

Briefly closing her eyes, she breathed in deeply and ordered herself to stop. The mild OCD had started a few years ago. She wasn't crazy. The ritual simply helped to relieve her stress. But she'd been trying to use breathing exercises to replace it.

"Look, I'll come for a weekend in January, okay?" Shea said, anticipating her mother's inevitable objection. "It'll be quieter then and we can spend more time together."

"That won't work for me."

"Sorry, Mom, it'll have to. We'll talk more later, all right? I have to go."

"But, Shea—"

She clenched her teeth together and forced herself to disconnect the call, acutely aware of how much she'd just royally ticked off her mother. And how desperately she needed a large number of deep breaths. But there was no other way. Shea would hate herself if she gave in now and backed out of volunteering. Not only that, but Rachel McAllister had also gone above and beyond to provide a room even though the ranch was closed for December.

As much as Shea hated having to impose, she was glad she

didn't have to mingle with other guests. Her interaction with the family would be minimal. She planned on being gone each morning before they sat down to breakfast and not returning until bedtime. The schedule suited her fine—she wanted to spend as much time at the shelter as she could. For her, animals were always easier to deal with than people.

"Hey, you."

At the sound of Nancy's voice, she brought her head up. The sharply dressed marketing director stood in the doorway, a black leather briefcase in one hand, a red designer purse nearly as big in the other.

"I thought everyone had left already," Shea said, wondering if any coworkers had overheard her phone conversation. They'd be surprised at her taking such a strong stand. But hey, she was the new Shea.

"The gang from Contracts went to O'Malley's pub. We're meeting them over there. Pack up and let's go."

"Oh." Shea shifted her gaze to her watch, the familiar squeeze of dread bringing her shoulders down. "Maybe next time. I still have some work to catch up on."

"Nobody works late this close to Christmas. Besides, tonight is trivia, and we need you on the team." Nancy's glossy peach lips lifted in challenge.

Shea stared helplessly at her monitor screen, biting her lip, trying to think of a graceful way out. She did enjoy the trivia, but the rest of it? It was difficult to be with a group like that, especially when they thought she had no sense of humor, and they called her Spock. She was sure they thought it was funny, but just because she was different didn't mean she didn't have feelings.

"Hey." Sympathy warmed Nancy's eyes. "You love showing up all those nerds from accounting."

One victory was enough for the day, although she appreciated the invitation. "Another time, okay?"

"If you change your mind…"

She wouldn't. She rarely did.

2

HER HANDS CRAMPED from holding the steering wheel so tightly, Shea saw the sign indicating the Sundance Ranch and drove her rented SUV down the gravel driveway. The sky was overcast, the nearby mountaintops covered with snow, but fortunately there was none on the ground.

Thank God.

She'd forgotten about the whole snow issue. Her adult life had been spent in California and only twice had she driven in anything worse than a good downpour. When the rental agent had assured her that the Toyota was equipped with snow tires and four-wheel drive, but asked if she knew how to put chains on her tires, she'd about had a stroke. Only then did she consider that she should've researched Montana weather before committing to the shelter.

That was the kind of obvious stuff that went clear over her head. She was like her father in that regard. A soaring IQ and not enough common sense. No, her father won that round—at least Shea hadn't married someone she'd known for only two minutes.

A bunch of buildings came into view but it was the house that Shea focused on. She remembered the description from the website and knew the original log cabin had been two stories, was over a hundred and fifty years old and various renovations and additions over the generations had expanded the residence.

Still, knowing what she did hadn't prepared her. The place was huge, three stories with two separate wings, the front of the house facing the Rockies. As she got closer she saw the windows, large expanses of glass that would allow perfects views.

Spirals of smoke rose from the dark green roof and disappeared into the gray sky. There were at least three fireplaces going. She loved fireplaces for the crackling sound burning wood made and for toasting marshmallows. But this wasn't really a vacation, she reminded herself, and she had no intention of imposing on the family. When she wasn't at the shelter she'd be sticking to her room. The McAllisters had been good enough to take her in when they should be celebrating the holidays alone, as a family. That's what this time of year was for.

Or so she'd been told a time or two. She had no practical experience in the matter. Even when her parents had been married, the atmosphere at home hadn't been particularly cozy. Her father was a workaholic and her mother a shopaholic. Shea had gotten a lot of studying done. Later, when she'd been sent to boarding school, she hadn't minded at all. Going home for the holidays? That hadn't always worked out so well.

There seemed to be two areas for parking, one closer to the house, the other a grassy brown spot next to a large building that was probably the stables. She slowed the SUV, then saw a young woman step outside onto the porch that wrapped around both corners of the house.

Bundled in a green down jacket, the auburn-haired woman, who Shea would bet was Rachel, smiled and waved. After gesturing for Shea to park on the grass, she rubbed her hands together and blew on them before stuffing them into the pockets of her worn jeans.

Behind her the front door opened again. Another woman—older, shorter—appeared, followed by a tall man with longish dark hair. Shea couldn't see him clearly, for one thing she was too busy parking and trying not to demolish the building. Plus, her pulse had sped up and her hands had grown clammy.

What was this, the welcoming committee? It was hard enough meeting strangers and now she felt as if she were suddenly on a stage. Maybe it was a dude ranch tradition…the whole family greeting the new guest. She shuddered. Weird. This was precisely why staying at a B and B had never appealed to her. People expected conversation and small talk. Definitely not her strong suit.

Bracing herself, she put the SUV in Park and turned off the ignition. She grabbed her purse and opened the door. The sound of an engine confused her for a second. She looked at the keys in her hand.

The noise was coming from behind, she realized, and twisted around to see that a huge black pickup had followed her down the driveway. With the windows rolled up and the heater going, she hadn't heard it. The driver parked closer to the house and it was quickly apparent that Shea wasn't the reason everyone had rushed to the porch, and she had to laugh at her own paranoia. At least she could see the humor in it now. Climbing out of the car, she smiled as the younger woman approached her and the other two converged on the truck.

"Shea Monroe, right?" she said, grinning, and Shea nodded. "I'm Rachel. We spoke when you made your reservation." The woman extended her hand.

"Yes, I remember." Shea started to pull off her glove but Rachel stopped her.

"Don't. It's freezing." Rachel laughed and squeezed Shea's gloved hand. "At least I had enough sense to grab my jacket."

"Thanks again for giving me a room. I swear I'll be no trouble."

"Hey, we're big supporters of Safe Haven. It's so nice of you to give up your holidays to volunteer. My brother works with them quite a bit and occasionally we foster horses."

Shea's gaze automatically went to the man and the older woman who stood beside the truck. He was very nice-looking, about her age, she guessed.

"That's Trace over there with our mom," Rachel said. "He's one of the hooligans but not the one I was talking about." The new arrivals, a man and a woman, stepped out of the truck and Rachel waved frantically at them. "That's my other brother Cole and his girlfriend, Jamie. He just picked her up at the airport. She's come to spend Christmas with us."

"Oh, you have two brothers. How nice," Shea said, and when Rachel gave her a quizzical look she just smiled. No, she wasn't a sparkling conversationalist, so better everyone know now.

"I have three." Rachel studied her a moment. "You probably noticed them on the website…."

"Oh, right." She wasn't in the habit of lying, but having noticed her brothers seemed to mean something to Rachel so Shea didn't see the harm in the small fib.

Rachel titled her head slightly to the side, amusement dancing in her bright green eyes. "Or maybe not. It doesn't matter. I'll help with your bags and then you can meet everyone."

"No, please, go be with your family. I'll be along in a minute."

"No worries. I'll see them later." Rachel swung around to the back of the SUV. "How many bags? I can get Trace to—"

"That's not necessary," Shea said, cutting her off then feeling ashamed for being rude. She cleared her throat. "Thanks, but I don't have much and I need to do some rearranging before I come in." She paused. "If that's okay?"

"Sure. I didn't mean to rush you. Take all the time you need." Rachel lightly touched her arm, the understanding in her eyes a bit unnerving. "We can be a boisterous bunch, but I promise we don't bite."

Shea managed a grateful nod before Rachel turned away, then felt her face flame. She hated the random attacks of shyness that plagued her when she was around too many people. Quickly, she opened the back hatch and busied herself with sifting through her suitcase. A few things, such as her heavy boots and mittens, could stay in the back of the car. No sense lugging them back and forth to the house. She'd need them at the shelter, not here.

Her gaze drifted toward the animated group as they chatted and laughed, grabbing luggage and totes full of wrapped presents from the back of the truck. Cole was tall and dark like Trace, with hair that brushed his collar. And the honey-blonde woman, Cole's girlfriend, was very pretty. She seemed comfortable with the family, as if she'd known them for a long time.

Shea couldn't help but be a little envious of the lively group. The men not so much, but the three women were gabbing as if there wasn't enough time to get everything in. Good for them. But being an outsider was fine with her. Comfortable. Familiar.

She had the strangest feeling that someone was watching her and turned to scan the outer building. An indistinct rider was galloping in from the south. Appearing oblivious to the cold, a pair of beautiful roans munched hay from a bale in the corral. It was close to dinnertime so she wasn't surprised that there were no workers in sight. The only other sign of humanity was smoke streaming out of the smokestack of one of the brick-and-wood buildings, probably the bunkhouse.

She started to turn back to sorting when she saw him under the archway to the barn. She'd almost missed him, standing in the shadows, lean and tall—well over six feet. He wore faded jeans, a brown flannel shirt, boots and work gloves, and he stared out, though not at her. His attention was on the family, who now headed toward the front steps.

She couldn't seem to tear her gaze away from him. He could've been a McAllister. He had the same coloring, the height, the same dark hair as the two brothers, except his was much shorter, almost a military cut. But that wasn't what made her doubt he was one of the brothers, it was the way he held himself back from the group. Like an outsider idly looking on…like she had.

Maybe he was one of the hired hands. Very good-looking, at any rate. Just an observation. It wasn't that she was interested. She was totally done with men. They weren't worth the aggravation. Even sex was overrated in her opinion. Focusing on her work gave her far more satisfaction. And she hoped her time at the shelter would help fill her need to connect with another living, breathing being. Preferably a horse. She loved horses, always had.

Shea smiled as she thought about all the childhood letters she'd written to Santa asking for a pony. But all she'd ever gotten were silly froufrou dresses from her mother and educational toys from her father. Oh, and that trip to Disneyland when she was nine. Her parents had argued the entire time and divorced three months later.

A week after her father had moved out of the house, Shea had asked for a dog, but her mother had refused what she deemed an "added burden." It had probably been for the best. The way Shea had accelerated though prep school and then college, she'd never really had time to care for a pet. But she was seriously considering adopting a dog now. She still worked ungodly hours, but maybe she could trade her corner office for a kennel on the first floor. After all, other employees were provided day care for their kids.

The family had disappeared inside and the man from the barn had disappeared, too. If she didn't hurry, she knew Rachel would send someone after her. Shea swung her suitcase out of the back, then hurried toward the porch. All she wanted was for someone to point out her room, where she could hibernate until it was time to head to the shelter in the morning.

JESSE STOMPED the dried dirt off his boots outside the mudroom door, then entered the small space that led to the kitchen. His eyes were gritty and he still hadn't gotten all the filth off his hands even though he'd been wearing gloves and had washed up some in the barn. He didn't care. Manual labor was exactly what he'd needed. His back and shoulder muscles were pleasantly sore and just maybe he'd get a full night's sleep.

"Good. You're here," Rachel said before he'd opened the kitchen door all the way. She ran her gaze down the front of his shirt and jeans and wrinkled her nose. "What have you been doing?"

"Cleaning out the barn shed. We had too much equipment packed in there."

"God. Go take a shower. We have guests."

"Jamie will be here a whole week. And she came to see Cole, not us."

"I wasn't thinking only of Jamie but of Shea, too." Rachel opened the oven and the spicy smell of lasagna filled the kitchen.

His stomach growled. "What about her?"

"Cool the attitude. It's not as if she's a regular guest," Rachel said, throwing him an annoyed look while pulling on oven mitts. "She's going to be at the shelter most of the time and only here to sleep. So if you're still pissy about me taking her in, get over it."

"I don't care who's here. I doubt I'll be around much myself."

The sudden hurt in Rachel's eyes made him look away. She said nothing, but concentrated on taking the steaming dish out of the oven.

"I'll go take that shower," he murmured and kept walking.

"Jesse?"

He wanted to ignore her. He wished he hadn't made that unnecessary crack about not being around. "What do you want, squirt?"

She didn't react to the hated childhood nickname. "It's almost Christmas. You know how much the holidays mean to Mom."

"I'm not gonna mess anything up, okay?"

"Not on purpose you wouldn't."

Sighing, he briefly closed his eyes and rubbed them with the heels of his hand. "What do you want from me, Rachel? I cut down the trees for the living room and the den, strung the lights along the eves. I'm here. I'm participating."

Except he wasn't really here, not emotionally. That's what Rachel was getting at, even though she managed to give him a small smile. "I know, Jesse. You've been great about helping us decorate. You have far more patience than Cole or Trace for that sort of thing."

He tugged at a tendril of hair that had escaped her ponytail. "Shower first, then I'll help set the table."

"I have something else I'd rather you do," she said quickly.

"What's that?"

"Shea is staying in the guest wing. First room on the right. Knock on her door and tell her dinner will be ready in ten."

He opened his mouth to refuse, then just nodded. Hell, he didn't have to be in a hospitable mood to knock on a door.

"And don't take no for an answer," Rachel added, wagging a wooden spoon at him. "I'm holding you responsible."

Jesus, his sister could be a pain in the ass. He waved her off, headed out of the kitchen and took the stairs two at a time to the second floor. Voices and laughter came from the den and he thought about yanking Trace away to go get the woman. But that wouldn't be fair. Besides, once he showed his face he'd have to acknowledge Jamie, then make small talk.

It wasn't that he didn't like Cole's girlfriend—he did. He was glad they'd hooked up. His brother couldn't have done better. But there would be enough time for socializing at dinner. The forty minutes of mindless pleasantries seemed to be as much as Jesse could handle lately.

He'd peeled off his clothes, showered and shampooed in nine minutes, then stood at the woman's door, trying like hell to recall her name. Didn't matter. Basically, he was only delivering a message.

She answered his knock immediately, warily pulling open the door a few inches and regarding him with surprised gray-blue eyes. She blinked, did a quick survey of his flannel shirt and jeans, then met his eyes again. "Oh, it's you."

"Um..." He stepped back. "I don't think we've met."

Blinking again, she opened the door a little more, enough for him to see that she also wore jeans and that her feet were bare. "I saw you earlier." She moved the long bangs away from her eyes. "Are you Rachel's brother?"

Jesse nodded and almost smiled at the trim woman. Straight off, there was something different about her. Unlike so many of the females who'd been guests at the ranch, she hadn't been artful or flirty with her hair, she'd just shoved it out of the way. "Dinner's ready," he said, disengaging from her forthright stare to get a better look.

Shea held herself tall even though she wasn't. He'd guess five-six? A little thin, but no big deal. While her body was pleasant, he was drawn back to her face, her unusual eyes with their dark lashes. He liked that she had full lips but didn't wear a hint of lipstick on them. He might not mind the look of the gloss, but he'd never liked the taste.

"Uh," she said, shaking her head, her straight light brown hair swinging from side to side and bringing him back to the conversation. "I'm not eating with you."

He didn't know what to say at first and just stared as she pressed her lips together, making one cheek dimple. "Should I take this personally?"

"No," she said matter-of-factly. "I promised Rachel I wouldn't be any trouble. I have some cheese crackers here. . . ." A slight frown puckered her brows. "There's no rule against eating in the rooms, is there?"

"I doubt it." Jesse laughed. "Look, Rachel made lasagna. If you don't come down, she'll be charging up to get you. Not to mention I'll get chewed out."

"Hmm, this is a bit awkward," she said, with a frank unwavering gaze he found intriguing. "Honestly, I didn't think this would be an issue."

He moved farther back to give her space. "For now how about coming downstairs with me? I can smell the lasagna from here."

She sniffed, and her stomach growled loudly. She glanced down with annoyance and pressed a hand to her flat belly. "I haven't had home cooking in a long time, and you're right, it smells heavenly."

"My sister can be a pain in the neck, but I'll admit, the woman can cook."

She flashed him a quick smile. "I'm Shea, by the way. Did you tell me your name?"

He shrugged. "It's Jesse."

"Pleased to meet you, Jesse." She offered her hand in an unexpected businesslike manner.

"Likewise." He liked her firm grip, the softness of her palm pressed against his. "I hear Rachel rounding up everyone."

"What?"

"I think dinner is on the table."

"Okay." She released his hand and dragged her palm down the front of her jeans. She slipped through the doorway into the hall, still barefoot.

"No one will care whether you're wearing shoes or not, but you should know we have wood floors downstairs."

Shea looked down. "Oh." She grinned and wiggled her toes. When she lifted her gaze, her cheeks were slightly flushed, making her eyes seem a little bluer. "I forgot. You go ahead if you want. I'll be right there."

He watched her disappear into her room but didn't move except to fold his arms across his chest, lean against the wall and wait. The irony of him being the one Rachel sent as the family's goodwill ambassador wasn't lost on him. He of all people couldn't blame anyone for not wanting to sit around with a bunch of strangers and he'd be the last person coaxing someone to the table.

Yeah, he'd considered backing off, letting her eat her crackers in peace. But he didn't think Shea's reluctance was due to shyness or anything other than genuinely not wanting to intrude. What a change from most of the guests who'd come to stay since Rachel started the dude ranch six months ago.

Some of those women had been something else. Even Trace, who was quite the Casanova, had started complaining about finding them under every rock. Not that it mattered to Jesse. He'd usher Shea downstairs and that would be it. If he had a rescue to deliver, maybe he'd see her at the shelter. And if not, that was fine, too.

3

When Shea saw all the people sitting at the large dining-room table she wanted to turn around and run. Of course the whole family would be here. What was she thinking agreeing to have dinner with them? She'd let her empty tummy sway her.

"Here, Shea." Rachel pulled out a chair. "Sit next to me. I'll introduce you to everyone."

They were all looking at her with friendly expressions but that didn't help. Her pulse had already started racing, her legs felt leaden and stiff and she was pretty much stuck because she doubted she could make it up the stairs.

She nearly jumped out of her skin when she felt the pressure of a hand at the small of her back. She whipped her head around and met Jesse's warm brown eyes.

"Go ahead," he said, with an encouraging smile—he must have noticed how tense she was. That knowledge didn't help one bit. "I'll get you something to drink. Wine?"

She jerked her chin in some vague form of a nod and kept her focus on the empty chair until she was safely seated.

No one seemed to have observed her attack of nerves, no one except Jesse, of course. Rachel had already started passing a platter of bread and butter around the table.

"Listen up, everyone," she said, pulling a large glass bowl

of salad toward her. "This is Shea. I lied and told her how nice and perfectly civilized we all are, so try and fake it, okay?"

Laughter interspersed with indignation filled the room. The older woman Shea had seen earlier sat at the head of the table shushing them, then directed a smile at Shea. "I'm Barbara McAllister, the mother of this rowdy bunch. Except Jamie over there, who I've decided to claim, anyway."

Grinning, the blonde lifted a hand and wiggled her fingers.

"That's Cole cutting the lasagna," Barbara continued.

"Glad you could join us, Shea," he said, regarding her with the same dark eyes as Jesse. "Hand me your plate. I've got a nice big juicy piece for you."

"Come on, you know I have a system." Rachel stopped tossing the greens to glare at her brother. "Keep cutting. Let me get the salad passed around clockwise and then—"

"Oh, Christ, here we go—"

"Trace!" Barbara gave him a reproving look.

A giggle rose in Shea's throat and she pressed her lips together trying to smother the sound.

Rachel clearly heard. "What?" she asked, her mouth slightly curved. "It's okay. Everyone laughs at Trace."

"No, your system. Passing clockwise," Shea said, trying to compose herself. "I get that. I really do."

"Thank you," Rachel said with a smug lift of her chin aimed at Trace.

He made a crack that Shea didn't hear because Jesse came up behind her, and suddenly all her senses were fixated on him.

"Would you like white or red?" he asked, bending close to her ear, his warm breath tickling her skin and sending an unexpected shiver down her spine.

She turned her head and saw that he was holding a bottle of wine in each hand. "Actually, I'm not much of a drinker. Maybe I should stick with water."

"All right, but this chardonnay is pretty good stuff." His voice was low and deep, and terribly unnerving because it seemed meant only for her.

Shea sighed. Probably a mistake given that she was already feeling rather warm, but she said, "Maybe a little."

"Wine?" Trace snorted. "What's the occasion?"

"Think, you heathen. We're celebrating Jamie coming to be with us for the holidays." Rachel sprinkled sunflower seeds on the salad, gave it a long approving look, then passed the bowl to her mother.

Jamie grinned. "We can always hook you up to a keg, Trace."

"Hey, I'm down with that." Trace smiled, his teeth strikingly white against his tan skin.

He was one of those real charmers, Shea thought, watching the way he casually combed his fingers through his thick dark hair. Probably had a string of girlfriends.

Shea forgot all about Trace as Jesse leaned in between her and Rachel to pour them each some wine. He brushed her shoulder as he maneuvered his upper body through the narrow space. Angled toward Shea, his flat belly only inches away, he ignited a tingling, nervous sensation that made her hold her breath and force her face straight.

One, two, three...four, five, six...seven, eight, nine...

His task accomplished, he retreated, and she stopped counting, unclenched her teeth and let out a slow breath that was still a bit shaky.

"Thank you," she managed to say in a small voice.

"You're welcome." He'd already moved on to his mother, poured red for her and then continued on, filling everyone else's glasses.

Okay, that was weird. Not her reaction—she always hated when anyone got too close—but the heat spreading through her limbs unsettled her some. Jeez, was she ever regretting the dinner invitation. This was torture and to top it off, her appetite was gone.

She hadn't realized she was still tracking him until she heard her name and it was clear someone was trying to get her attention.

Blinking, she glanced around the table and saw Mrs. McAllister smiling at her.

"It's so good of you to give up the holidays with your family to volunteer at Safe Haven," she said. "The people there are wonderful and I'm sure they appreciate your sacrifice."

"Oh, it's no sacrifice." Shea realized how that sounded, picked up her wineglass and took a sip. "I wanted to get away for the holidays."

"I did, too." Jamie accepted the bowl of salad from Trace and heaped some on her plate. "I don't have any brothers and sisters, and my parents live in Zurich, so I'm glad the McAllisters took pity on me."

"Excuse me." Cole stopped serving lasagna to lift an eyebrow at her. "Is that your only reason for coming?"

Even as the corners of Jamie's mouth quirked, her forehead creased in a confused frown. "I can't think of anything else," she said with an exaggerated innocence that even Shea could tell was a fake.

"Zap!" Trace barked out a laugh. "How's your ego, bro?"

Jamie leaned over and kissed Cole half on the mouth and half on the cheek, her hand reaching under the table.

"I'd shut up until I got my lasagna if I were you," Rachel told Trace.

"If you were me you'd be smarter and better-looking."

"Oh, God." Rachel rolled her eyes. "Mom, are you sure you didn't find him on the side of the road?"

"You're all hopeless." Barbara McAllister shook her head, but it was clear she didn't mind her children horsing around.

Jesse smiled at the teasing as he took his seat but he

seemed to be the most serious of the bunch. Shea thought back to when she first saw him, standing apart from the rest of the family. He hadn't rushed to greet Jamie, though Shea had a feeling his reticence had nothing to do with the woman.

The salad finished making its round. Everyone but Shea had taken a slice of bread, which looked homemade. Plates were passed to receive the cheesy pasta, but not to Rachel's satisfaction because she complained her system had been ruined.

Shea liked her. A lot. She liked Jamie, too, because Shea had the impression that Jamie had chimed in to bail her out.

It was odd for her to take a liking to anyone so quickly. Her gaze drifted to Jesse. She kind of liked him, too, but she hated that he was sitting directly across from her. It was difficult not to stare at him.

His hair was still a little damp on top, but the sides were so short they were already dry. The conservative cut made her think he'd be the clean-shaven type, but he'd left the stubble of beard that shadowed his jaw and chin. That and his tanned skin gave him a rugged look. She found the combination oddly appealing.

Rachel must have passed Shea's plate to Cole without her seeing because it was now heaping with a portion she'd never be able to finish. It smelled divine, though, and with her renewed appetite she was willing to give it her best try.

For a few minutes it was quiet while everyone dug in to their meals. Ignoring the tempting aroma of the lasagna, she started with her salad because that's what she always did. She'd finished chewing a cherry tomato when Rachel turned to her.

"So, Shea, do you ride?" she asked.

She dabbed the corners of her mouth with her napkin. "A

little. I took refresher lessons last week, but I don't think that's a requirement of the shelter."

"Oh, no, I didn't mean to imply that. I thought you might enjoy a trail ride tomorrow. We have a couple of very gentle mares in our stables, and since it's your only free day before you start at Safe Haven—"

"I don't have a free day. I start tomorrow. But thank you for your offer."

Frowning, Rachel put down her fork. "I thought Annie Sheridan said she would be giving the volunteers their orientation."

Shea had the name of her contact written down but she was fairly certain it was Annie. "Yes, I believe she's the person I spoke to."

"That's odd. She told me she had three volunteers answer her ad and they all started on Monday. Maybe I'm wrong. Forget I said anything."

Panic squeezed Shea's chest. Had she mixed up the dates? It was possible. She'd been in such a hurry. Tomorrow was Sunday. Oh, God, why hadn't she stopped to consider this was the weekend and starting on Monday made much more sense?

The sudden lapse into silence flustered her. Not only that, but she also just knew everyone was staring at her. She refused to look up but concentrated on spearing another cherry tomato. She'd promised to stay out of the family's way. They were probably wondering why she'd arrived a day early.

"I think I'll drive over there tomorrow, anyway." She gave a small shrug. "Maybe they could still use some help."

"Actually, I think Annie's in Kalispell picking up supplies," Rachel said quietly. "It's really the perfect time for a trail ride." She paused. "I can take you myself."

Oh, how Shea wished the beautiful finished wood floor

would simply part and swallow her whole. This was so typical of her. Couldn't even keep a date straight.

JESSE CHEWED his food and took a quick sip of wine to wash it down. It wasn't like Rachel to be insensitive. Why the hell didn't she lay off? Couldn't she see that Shea was embarrassed? The poor woman could barely look up.

"I'll take you," he said, keeping his gaze on her, knowing that everyone else's attention abruptly turned to him. "I have to inspect some fencing along the north pasture. Won't take long, then we can head over to Lincoln Pass. That is, if you're interested."

Her anxious eyes met his. "I don't want to be any trouble," she said softly.

"I have to go, anyway." He shrugged. "It's beautiful country, when it's not buried under ten feet of snow. Even then, it's something to see."

"You should go," Rachel said, laying a hand on Shea's arm. "Between the weather and your duties at the shelter, tomorrow may be your only chance." She smiled. "I could pack you guys a picnic lunch."

He wanted like hell to nail his well-intentioned sister with a don't-push-it glare but he couldn't risk Shea seeing it. "Maybe we could work the ride around lunchtime," he said, fully intending to pull Rachel aside later. He didn't want her to read too much into his offer.

"I know the area Jesse's talking about," Jamie said. "It's breathtaking and you shouldn't miss it. Rachel, pass the bread, will you?"

Everyone went back to eating and talking, the subject turning to the open house later in the week. The event wasn't a big deal. His mother had been hosting it since they were kids, but Jamie had never been, and Rachel was describing the traditional menu and how piñatas filled with candy and small toys were hung for the children.

Shea concentrated on her food, smiling graciously when she was ordered to come home hungry the night of the open house. Jesse had the feeling she'd have preferred to be anywhere else right now. She sure wouldn't be showing her face at the party. Not that he blamed her. He'd do just about anything to get out of it himself. He wasn't feeling particularly cheerful about the holidays.

He'd recognized from the first that Shea had some shyness issues. Could be that she was avoiding her own family for Christmas and preferred to be alone. In any case, he doubted she'd want to rub elbows with a bunch of strangers. Nosy ones at that. Half the town would show up at the open house and they'd be curious about her since Rachel hadn't accepted any other guests.

"Isn't that right, Jesse?"

He looked at his mother, at a total loss. "Sorry, what was that?"

She smiled. "Never mind, son. Eat your supper."

He didn't ask again. The guarded way his brothers were eyeing him, he figured she'd made yet another remark about how good it was to have him back. Although he'd never said anything, they knew it irritated him. This time of year she tended to be more sentimental. They'd lost their father to cancer eleven years ago, and she still missed him. They all did.

Sometimes he still felt guilty for having worried her by joining the air force. It made no sense. He hadn't asked to be shipped out. He'd merely done his duty and enlisted, the same as every other McAllister male before him. But if he reenlisted now…

Shit, he couldn't think about what would happen to her if she lost a son, too. His decision had to be based on what was best for the whole family and the survival of the Sundance.

He stabbed at a piece of lasagna, determined to enjoy his meal and block the litany of concerns plaguing his mind. Yeah, he had to make a decision soon, just not this week. For now he needed to be the good son, the amenable brother. Rachel was more than pulling her weight by running the dude ranch and he'd help out by taking her guest for a lousy trail ride. It was the least he could do.

Instead of taking a bite he grabbed his wineglass, and as he brought it to his lips, he looked across at Shea. She glanced up at the same time, her soft gray eyes tinged with something close to gratitude.

Hell, he hoped she didn't get the wrong idea. His offer was meant to make life easier for Rachel. It had nothing to do with Shea. Nothing at all.

IT WAS THE ALTITUDE making her feel a bit drugged. Shea struggled to inhale the cold thin air deep into her lungs and shuddered. She'd obviously disturbed Gypsy because the gentle mare took the next two steps high and Shea squeezed her thighs around the animal's girth, afraid she was about to slide backward out of the saddle.

A few feet ahead of her, Jesse turned around, his brown Stetson pulled low to block the sun. "You okay?"

"Fine."

Only when he lowered his gaze to her hand did she realize she was gripping the saddle horn. She released it and forced herself to relax. The sky was clear and blue, the side of the mountain covered with a beautiful array of pine trees in varying shades of green. Back home when it was cold the sky was usually gray and the air damp, making everything seem dreary.

"Want to stop for a while?" Jesse slowed down until he rode abreast of her. They'd ridden that way most of the past hour, but he'd gone up ahead when they started the slight as-cent and the trail narrowed. "We can also turn around. Your call."

"Don't you have to check some fencing?"

He smiled and adjusted his hat. "That'll only take a minute."

She really appreciated him making time to ride with her. Last night she'd considered rejecting his offer, but it was good practice and the last chance she'd have to get comfortable in the saddle. "I'd like to keep going."

He ran his gaze down the front of her pink down jacket, then followed her jean-clad leg to the boot she had tucked into the stirrup. Naturally he couldn't see anything interesting but the scrutiny made her tingle, anyway. "What are you wearing under that?"

"Excuse me?"

The skin at the corners of his eyes crinkled and his mouth lifted in a vague smile. "You should have thermal underwear. You'll be working outside a lot at Safe Haven."

"Guess I should've thought of that. I'll go to town later."

He reached over and casually caught her hand, startling her. "You have another pair of gloves?" he asked, inspecting the inside fleece lining.

"These are quite warm."

"Waterproof?"

"Um, not sure."

"They should have a snug closure around here," he said, showing her by closing his large hand around the glove and her wrist. "Keeps the cold air from getting in there."

"I see what you mean." Her hand did feel warmer. In fact a toasty flush surged through her entire body. Apparently she'd been spending too much time staring at his broad shoulders instead of the scenery.

He let go at the same time as she pulled her hand away. "The shelter might have an extra pair you can use, but if not

I can loan you my old work gloves. They're too big so you'd have to wear them over yours."

"Thanks, but I'm sure I can find something suitable in town."

"Maybe. You have small hands and inventory is low to make room for Christmas gifts and decorations. But try Abe's Variety or the hardware store."

"I will." She smiled, turning to take in the scenery, feeling a little shy all of a sudden. Odd, because although she didn't like being around people as a general rule, especially after Brian, she tended to dismiss men altogether. But with Jesse…her off button seemed to be malfunctioning.

With a mixture of relief and disappointment she saw that the path was again narrowing and they'd have to return to single file. She waited for him to speed up.

"You go on ahead," he said. "I'm not worried about overhanging branches up here."

She clicked her tongue and after a gentle nudge, Gypsy trotted ahead of Jesse and his beautiful black gelding. The incline wasn't too bad but where the snow had been patchy only five minutes ago, the higher they climbed the more it obscured the rocky path.

The truth was, it made her nervous. She wouldn't complain, though. It was winter and this was Montana, so if she'd given it the kind of thought it deserved, instead of spacing out, she would have expected a lot more snow, actually. Though the mountaintops were certainly packed solid.

They rode in silence for another five minutes and then Jesse said, "There's a meadow not far from here. We'll stop there, water the horses and see what kind of snacks Rachel packed for us."

"I told her not to go to the trouble…." Shea twisted around to look at him, letting out a yelp when she nearly lost her balance.

She clung tightly to the reins but she'd already spooked Gypsy. The mare reared slightly. Shea held on for all she was worth.

In seconds Jesse was standing beside her, whispering to the horse, calming her, one hand stroking her neck. Shea stayed as still as she could, even when he switched from petting the horse to petting her arm.

4

JESSE CLENCHED his jaw. He was an ass for bringing her up here. His intentions had been good. The view was spectacular from this vantage point. But he should've taken into account that she might not be an experienced enough rider. Hell, it seemed as if he couldn't do one stinkin' thing right these days.

"You okay?" he asked, rubbing her trembling arm.

"I'm fine. Embarrassed, but I'll survive." She shifted away from his touch, and he backed off.

"Let's stop for a while." He swung out of the saddle and offered her a hand down.

Shea resisted his help, her determination to stay mounted plain in her flushed face. "Is Gypsy mad? Does she want me off?"

"Mad?" He smiled. "Don't think so. I figured you might want to take a break. And for the record, no reason to be embarrassed."

She moistened her rosy lips. They looked chapped. "I'd rather we get to where we're going."

He stroked the mare's flank, while scanning the scraggly brush and thicket of pine trees for any sign of a predator. Gypsy was a gentle horse and it wasn't like her to spook that easily. Yet she'd be whinnying and trying to run if there was a hungry cougar nearby. And Rambo wouldn't be calmly munching the tall dead grass after Jesse had dismounted.

"Okay," he said, giving the bay a final rub down her rump. "We'll go slow. We're in no hurry."

"I panicked and jerked the reins. It was all me."

"Don't worry about it." He lifted his hat, then reset it on his head and let out a low whistle. "Come on, Rambo."

"What did you call him?" She glanced over her shoulder but kept her body rigidly forward. "What's your horse's name?"

He rarely thought about the silly name anymore, not unless someone brought it up. "Rambo."

"Oh. Are you a fan of the movie?"

"My little brother named him." Jesse swung up into the saddle, then with his heel tapped the horse's flank to get him moving. "Trace was nine when Rambo was given to me as a colt, and I promised to let him choose the name."

"That's sweet."

"Yeah, well, I threatened to change it at least a dozen times."

"But you didn't."

He shrugged a shoulder even though she couldn't see him. She was concentrating on getting past a snowdrift, while Jesse focused on the slim curve of her hips. She needed a longer jacket. And not so pink. Jesus, she could attract a half-blind predator with no sense of smell.

Sticking to a slow pace, he let the horses pick their way over the rocks single file. The path wasn't dangerous or he wouldn't have brought Shea this way, but he could tell she was a little nervous and for that he regretted taking this route. She obviously wasn't the outdoors type, and he shouldn't have made the assumption she was just because she'd volunteered to work at Safe Haven.

He wondered if she knew what she was in for. A large

animal sanctuary was different than a city shelter that took in dogs and cute little kittens. Annie Sheridan had run the place for the past two years and there wasn't a critter she'd turn down, whether it be an ornery mud-drenched sow or a pregnant goat with an appetite for human hair. The abandoned Nubian he'd dropped off in August had nearly scalped Annie. The damn goat was so big the staff called her Camel.

"How did you hear about Safe Haven?" he asked as soon as the path widened and Shea seemed more relaxed.

"The internet."

"Were you specifically looking in Montana?"

"No."

Jesse had to smile. The woman could never be accused of being too wordy. Since they'd left the ranch it seemed he started most conversations. Silence generally suited him. Folks considered him the quietest of the three brothers and he couldn't recall meeting a woman who could match him in that department. Until now.

The differences between Shea and most of the guests who'd been coming to the Sundance were even more apparent since they'd met for the ride. Some of those women had been worse than coyotes stalking a calf separated from the herd. They had no compunction about letting a man know they were looking for vacation sex. Clearly they didn't understand that the chase was part of the fun. Last month one of them had pretended she'd caught him alone in the barn by accident. He'd given her high marks for playing the game with some smarts, but he still hadn't been interested. He didn't need any potential complications. Cole had met Jamie when she'd come to the ranch as a guest, but he was lucky. The whole thing could've gone sideways.

Jesse let Shea have her silence the few minutes it took to get to the meadow. Now that they were just below the snow line, there were only pockets of ice, but he figured this was still the nicest place around for them to eat. While he tethered the horses, he asked her to spread the blanket he kept in his saddlebag, then pour them coffee from the thermos while he dug out their snacks.

Taking her time, she made sure the ground was free of pebbles and twigs, then shook out the wool blanket and smoothed it all the way to the corners. Apparently the placement didn't meet with her approval because she rearranged it…twice. Then she stepped back with a critical eye, and bit at her lower lip.

When it looked as if she were going to start over, he stopped her. "You invite guests I don't know about?"

She blinked at him. "What?"

God save him from perfectionists. "It's fine, Shea."

She followed his gaze and stared at the blanket. "Oh. Right." Her cheek dimpled with her smile. "Don't worry. I'm not really crazy. A little compulsive, absentminded sometimes, but nothing certifiable." She rubbed her palms down the front of her jeans, then picked up the thermos and unscrewed the top.

"You mind me asking what you do for a living?"

She hesitated. "I'm a software engineer." She glanced around. "Do we have another cup?"

He rooted in the saddlebag for a tin cup he used when camping, wondering if that meant she was a computer jockey. "Here."

"I'll pour."

Holding the cup up to her, he watched while she focused on filling it within a quarter inch of the rim. "That's good."

"Oops, I should've asked if you'd be adding cream and sugar."

"Nope. I drink it black. So do you, so I didn't bring any."

"How did you know that?" she asked, staring at him and absently blowing the long bangs out of her eyes.

"Last night. After dinner." He took a quick sip. The warmth felt good going down. "You didn't use cream or sugar."

"Oh." She tilted her head to the side, as if mulling over what he'd said. "What do you do for a living?"

The question stopped him. Last time he'd been asked he was sitting in a bar in Vegas near Nellis Air Force Base. A blonde had sidled up to him and it was obvious she already knew he was a pilot before she'd opened her mouth. One fine thing about flying, you never had to be without a woman. But that night he'd lied, told her he was in data entry. She'd disappeared in seconds.

"I work at the ranch." He shrugged. "Doing whatever needs doing."

"I suppose that makes sense." She poured coffee for herself then seemed flustered that she didn't have a free hand to screw the thermos cap back on.

Jesse set his cup aside, took the thermos from her and completed the task. "You sound doubtful."

"Do I?" She pursed her lips. "Probably because you seem different than Cole and Trace."

"They look like real cowboys and I don't?"

Shea frowned thoughtfully. "That might be it."

He'd been teasing so that made him laugh.

"What?" She wrapped both hands around her cup and sipped, staring warily at him over the rim. She looked so earnest he had no idea what to make of her.

"Let's sit." He indicated the blanket she'd painstakingly spread. "I'm hungry."

She reached behind and rubbed her butt and lower back. "I think I'll stand."

He cringed inwardly at the pinched expression on her face. Probably his fault. "Too long in the saddle?"

"No, I just need to loosen up." She shivered. "And warm up."

"Here." He set down his coffee and unzipped his jacket.

"What are you doing?"

"Wear this. It'll help—"

"No." She moved back. "I'm not taking your jacket."

"I'll be okay."

"No, absolutely not." She retreated another step and coffee sloshed onto her hand.

He took the cup from her, then finished shrugging out of his jacket. "My fault. I should've made sure you were dressed appropriately to come up here."

"Please," she said tightly. "I'm not comfortable with this."

Jesse was the one to step back this time. He made sure there was plenty of space between them, wondering what she thought he was going to do. Jesus, he'd clearly given her the wrong idea.

"I'm sorry," he said, hooking the jacket onto his thumb and putting up both hands. "I didn't mean anything."

"No." Her eyes widened and her cheeks turned pink. "No, it's not you. It's just...I can't let you freeze because I hadn't planned well. I'd feel awful."

Relieved, he smiled. "Hey, I'm made of tough cowboy stock. I eat bullets for breakfast. I can take the cold."

"Put your jacket on," she said, with a small upward tilt of her lips. "Even your ears are red."

He touched them. Ice cold. The downside of wearing his hair so short. "Okay, this is how it's going to be...." He slid on his jacket but didn't zip it. Then he swooped up the blanket she'd carefully arranged. He shook off the clinging pebbles and dried leaves, folded the blanket in half and threw it around her shoulders.

"What—?" She tried to back up but he stopped her.

He gathered the ends together under her chin, aware that his fingers had brushed her breasts. The contact was innocent and unintentional, the down jacket thick enough that he didn't feel the need to apologize. That would make it worse.

"Come on," he said, pulling the blanket more snugly around her. "Doesn't this feel better?"

She shuddered again, huddled under the blanket and stared at him with eyes slightly wide, slightly confused. Her gloved hands slid over his to grasp the bunched wool. "Thank you."

"Got it?" he asked, then waited for her to nod before releasing his hold.

"Now we don't have anyplace to sit."

He zipped his jacket and indicated an outcropping of rocks close to the semifrozen stream. "How about over there?"

"If you'd rather, we can turn around."

"Is that what you want to do?"

She tilted her head back, her gaze lifted to the sky. She wore little makeup, if any, but then she didn't need anything. Her lashes were even thicker than he'd thought last night, and the more he looked into her gray-blue eyes, the more interesting they seemed. And her skin…it looked soft, really silky. Good thing he wasn't one to give in to impulse. He sure had a powerful itch to run his thumb across her cheek to see for himself.

"I love being out here. But I don't want to interfere with your work." She brought her small chin down and met his gaze. "I still can't believe I got my first day mixed up." She sighed. "That's a lie. I mess up timelines a lot."

"Here I figured you for the organized type."

"At work I am, but in my personal life…" She gave a small helpless shrug. "It seems I need to pay more attention to details."

Jesse threw out their cold coffee and poured them refills. "This time it worked out," he said, putting her cup in her hand.

"How do you mean?"

"You might not have had a chance to come up here. Isn't

it beautiful country?" He looked over the gently rolling hills that flattened out toward the Sundance.

Where the pine trees thinned, he could see the sun glistening off streams and creeks, which were partially iced over. Winter wasn't his favorite time of year, but the sagebrush and bunchgrass would be covered with snow soon and fields of undisturbed velvety white would produce a different kind of beauty. His chest tightened. Hard to think about leaving Montana. His family. The Sundance.

Damn, every time he figured he'd come to a decision, his thinking got muddled.

No, the problem wasn't so much in his head—his heart was doing the interfering. He knew better. There was no place for emotion in this debate. Duty came first.

"You're right. It's gorgeous." Silence again lapsed as she stood beside him, gazing out at the peaceful landscape. "Is that your ranch?" She pointed, and the blanket slid off her shoulders.

He caught it, but not before splashing coffee down the front of his jeans. "Son of a—" He cut himself short. "Sorry."

Looking horrified, she stared at his fly, or at least that's where her attention seemed to be centered. "I just keep being a nuisance."

"Hey, no problem. It'll freeze-dry in seconds." He paused. "My jeans."

"Right." She blushed. "I knew what you meant," she murmured, taking the blanket from him, and struggling with only one free hand to rearrange it around her hunched shoulders.

He wondered how old she was. She probably wasn't as young as he assumed. It wasn't just the blushing. Rachel blushed easily and she was a damn firecracker. Shea seemed...not naive necessarily, backward wasn't right, either...just different. Whatever it was, the woman had a strange effect on him he wasn't sure he cared for.

"I think we should go back. I still have to go to town for the thermal underwear and gloves, and I'd prefer to go before dark."

"You have a few hours—" he began, then saw a flicker of apprehension in her eyes. "You're right. Better to give yourself some extra time." He almost offered to drive her, but he had the impression she wanted to get away from him. He didn't take it personally. Maybe he should, though.

Different was one thing. *Interesting* was a whole new ball game. For his own sake, maybe she was someone he should stay away from, period.

JESSE MCALLISTER WAS gorgeous, his manners perfect and Shea loved the gentle way he talked to his horse. Any normal woman with a pulse would've noticed his dark good looks and quiet confidence. Apparently she could count herself among them, which was an oddity in itself. Her awareness level barely reached simmer when it came to the opposite sex. Any pubescent attraction she'd experienced had always been edged out by fear and awkwardness. She'd quickly learned to compartmentalize. It was quite remarkable that she'd even hooked up with Brian.

So what on earth was this fluttering sensation over Jesse? Because he was *nice?* Because he paid her some attention? God, she hoped not. That would make her too much like her mother.

Taking a deep breath, she tried to relax as he helped her into the saddle. He was merely being polite, she reminded herself. Her flustered reactions were her problem, not his. What made the situation more difficult was the whole touching thing. Jesse was so casual about brushing her arm, tucking the blanket around her shoulders, cupping the back of her lower calf to make sure her foot was anchored in the stirrup.

His hand had even accidentally grazed the front of her jacket earlier and he hadn't batted an eye.

"The wind has picked up. It'll be chilly riding back down. You ought to keep this around you." He offered the blanket, and as if reading her mind, added, "We'll take it nice and easy."

"Thank you," she said and exchanged Rambo's reins for the blanket.

Jesse swung up into his saddle and nudged the gelding into the lead. The horse hadn't advanced more than two feet when Jesse reined him in again. He eyed the struggle she was having with the blanket. Folding it in half made it more manageable as a shawl, but the wool was thick and heavy, and she was afraid she'd lose it halfway down the hill.

"Here." He leaned over and helped her arrange the blanket so that her shoulders and arms were covered, yet she could still keep a firm grip.

She sighed. "You must think I'm twelve."

He gave her that slow, easy smile of his. "Trust me, that's not what I think."

She didn't understand her reaction. It was physical, tense, but not like being trapped. And then there was the oddly pleasant apprehension in the pit of her stomach. Maybe it was the way his voice had lowered or the way his gaze roamed her face then lingered briefly on her lips. They *were* chapped. He was probably about to tell her to pick up some medicated balm while she was in town.

His eyes met hers, and he wasn't smiling anymore. "Ready?"

Nodding, she stared at the slight tic in his jaw and hoped she hadn't somehow annoyed him. She waited for him to go first and concentrated on clutching both the reins and the blanket. It was useless to try to figure out what had just happened. She was horrible at that sort of thing. Computer glitches? She was a whiz. But human glitches, she was better off ignoring.

When he reached the bottom of the slope he turned around and waited for her. That only made her more self-conscious and she wished he'd kept going. "Okay?" he asked.

"Fine."

"You can give Gypsy her head. She'll follow Rambo until we get to flatter ground."

Shea smiled.

"You still laughing at my horse's name?"

"It is funny."

"You're gonna hurt his feelings."

"With a name like Rambo? I don't think so."

Jesse laughed. It was a great sound. He leaned back and adjusted his hat while he watched her and Gypsy finish tackling the descent.

"You're making me nervous," she finally admitted. "Keep going. You don't have to wait."

"Yeah, I do, but I won't watch. How's that?" he said, amusement in his voice as he wheeled his horse around.

She darted a look from the rocky snow-dusted ground to his broad shoulders. "Not much better," she murmured.

"What was that?"

"Nothing." She held her breath until she and Gypsy were safely down the slope and standing beside Jesse.

He eyed the blanket that was again sagging off her back but he made no move to fix it. Crazily, she wished that he would. It was only curiosity, an experiment to see if she felt anything from him touching her again.

Her gaze was drawn to the shallow cleft in his chin, already dark with stubble. The flutter picked up, right behind her breastbone, and suddenly she was anxious to get back to the Sundance. To be in her car and away from the bewildering McAllisters.

Away from Jesse.

5

ARMED WITH BOTH a GPS and written directions, early the next morning Shea drove down the narrow bumpy highway toward Safe Haven. Sadly, she'd already finished the coffee from the to-go mug Rachel had fixed her. Although she would've loved more caffeine, the never-ending potholes and misty dimness around her were enough to keep her hands firmly gripping the wheel and her eyes wide and alert.

Only when she saw the sign for the Safe Haven turnoff did she feel comfortable reaching for the cheese crackers in her purse. She was starving. Last night's dinner had consisted of a diet cola she'd picked up in town along with her new gloves and thermal underwear. Rachel had tried to get her to join the family for dinner but Shea had refused, and while she'd turned down the full breakfast Rachel had offered, she had grabbed a warm muffin on the way out.

It wasn't about not being a bother anymore. She worried that it would've been awkward seeing Jesse. More than likely the problem was in her head. They'd had a perfectly nice ride yesterday. She couldn't have asked for a more courteous guide. They'd even talked a little on the way back. Nothing major, small talk, really… Which, come to think of it, was kind of major since she was so notoriously bad at it that she tried her best to keep to herself.

After inhaling the crackers, she nibbled away at her muffin as she searched for signs of the shelter. The land was flat out here to the east of town. There were a few trees and scrub brush but nothing like she'd seen on her ride with Jesse. At least it was easy to see what was coming up ahead, especially now that the sky was lightening up. She was licking the last crumbs from her fingers when she saw the big weathered barn. Two smaller wooden buildings sat off to the side, and Shea thought she could see the words *Safe Haven* etched on a plank stuck to a post.

Slowing the vehicle, she made the turn and pulled the rental alongside an old green pickup splattered with mud. Another truck was parked closer to the gate, but that was it, no sign anyone else was around. Of course, she was early.

"Welcome."

She heard someone calling to her even before she closed the car door.

"Over here. By the barn." The woman was tall and lean, her blond hair pulled into a long ponytail that swung back and forth as she waved her gloved hand. She wore badly faded jeans patched at the knees and a heavy brown parka that had a tear near the shoulder.

Shea acknowledged her with a reciprocal wave, then pocketed her keys. Deciding to leave her purse on the floorboard of the car, she met the woman halfway. "Are you Annie?"

"I am. And I bet you're one of our new volunteers." Annie pulled off a glove and extended her hand. "Shea Monroe, I'm guessing."

"You're right." Shea couldn't say why, but she'd expected someone older. Annie looked to be in her late twenties, maybe thirty, and so friendly that Shea didn't hesitate to shake the woman's hand.

"I cheated." Annie grinned. "The other two volunteers called to say they'd be an hour late."

"Ah." She smiled back, wondering if the Montana air had something to do with her newfound ease. "And here I'm early. Hope it isn't a problem."

"Are you kidding? I never turn down help with chores." She studied Shea for a moment, glancing at her jeans and boots. "I don't suppose you brought a pair of work gloves with you."

"Oh…I did." She dug the keys out of her pocket and used the remote to unlock the Toyota's rear door. The gloves were still in the package but she removed them, then used her teeth to break through the binding plastic ring. "I bought them in town yesterday. Jesse suggested I'd need something better than what I'd brought with me."

"Jesse?" Annie said, her brows arched in surprise.

"Jesse McAllister." Shea felt funny suddenly. Though she hadn't said anything wrong…she didn't think…. "I'm staying at the Sundance."

"That's right. Rachel mentioned it. You won't meet a nicer family."

"They've been wonderful. I hate that I'm imposing but I was desperate." She walked with Annie toward the barn, taking an extra step every few feet in order to keep up with Annie's mile-long legs.

"I've only known the McAllisters for two years, but I doubt you're intruding. Number one, they're very supportive of the shelter and are happy you're volunteering. And secondly, if you got Jesse to talk long enough to recommend gloves, then I'm sure they all love you to pieces." Annie stopped to pick up the bucket she'd left in the entryway of the barn. "If you don't mind, I'll wait until Molly and Hank, the other volunteers, arrive before I give a tour."

"Absolutely," Shea murmured, torn between being a bother and wanting to ask about Jesse.

"But I'm happy to have you come along while I feed the animals," Annie said. "The more exposure you have the better." Her kind blue eyes sparkled. "Now come meet Kiki. She'll be a little ornery at first but as soon as she gets some grain in her belly she'll be sweet as pie."

In a matter of seconds, Annie had flipped the moment's awkwardness into positive action. Envying the woman's ability, Shea followed in grateful silence as they entered a fenced-off section inside the cavernous barn. Hay was strewn across the hard dirt floor where chickens clucked around the hooves of grazing goats.

Shea had never seen a goat up close before and she was amazed at their varying sizes and how different they looked. She spotted a particularly tall brown-and-black one with big floppy ears who towered over the others and looked as if she might be the matriarch of the bunch. "Is that Camel?"

Annie slid her another curious look. "Jesse?"

She nodded. "He said she's partial to human hair."

"Never turn your back on her," Annie said. "Even if she's just eaten. It won't matter." She swung open the gate to a stall and a medium-size brown goat with tiny ears came trotting excitedly toward them. "This is Kiki, behind her is Angel."

Shea let out a delighted gasp at the still-gangly white baby goat that was smaller than a border collie. Except, like the brown goat, she practically had no ears. "She's adorable. How old is she?"

"About three weeks. They grow fast and they come out almost ready to walk. They're Lamanchas. That's why the small ears."

Even if Shea didn't know what was going on, apparently both goats knew what to do. She stood back to give them room and watched as they anxiously squeezed into the stall with an odd-looking wooden contraption. Kiki immediately jumped up onto the platform, stuck her head through something that might have been a neck harness and stared at the empty metal bowl sitting on a stump.

"Here you go, mama." Annie poured grain into the bowl, then latched the harness around Kiki's neck to keep her in place.

Angel had already jumped up onto the platform and started to nurse. Busy munching the grain, Kiki ignored the baby.

"Why do you have to lock her up like that?" Shea asked.

"So that she'll let Angel nurse and not hurt her. Kiki lost her two babies. She isn't Angel's mother and she won't allow her to nurse freely yet. It should happen eventually, but until then they have to be supervised." Annie tapped the wood contraption. "I use this as a milking station but it works well for this purpose. You volunteers will have Kiki and Angel on your duty list."

"Ouch!" Something yanked at Shea's hair and she jerked her head forward, her hand flying to the back of her scalp as she tried to tug free.

Annie quickly stepped in. "No," she ordered abruptly.

The pressure didn't ease and Shea felt a moment's panic. Suddenly she was released and she spun around to stare into the unconcerned brown eyes of Camel. The goat stared back, contentedly chewing…presumably a clump of Shea's newly washed hair. She rubbed the assaulted area of her scalp, expecting to find a bald spot, but everything seemed intact.

"Sorry about that." Annie gently shoved the goat's face aside. "Come on, Cami, beat it."

"Is that my hair she's chewing?"

"Alfalfa. I don't think she actually had time to do anything other than give you a good yank." Annie pressed her lips together, obviously trying not to laugh. "On the bright side, it's not likely to happen again."

"Oh, so that was an initiation."

"No, sadly, it's her favorite pastime, but I'm betting you never turn your back on her again."

"Um—" Shea smiled ruefully "—I wouldn't put money on that."

Annie eyed her a moment and then switched her gaze to Angel. The small goat reared back on her hind legs and used her front hooves to give Kiki's bulging udder a couple of whacks. Shea braced herself for the fallout, but Kiki, completely indifferent, kept eating her grain.

"Angel's not hurting her," Annie explained. "She's just getting the milk to flow better. It's instinctive."

Fascinated, Shea continued to watch. "I wish I knew more. I hope I'm not useless around here."

"No worries. We'll show you everything you need to know. I can't tell you how much we appreciate you volunteering. If not for people like you no one would have time to spend with their families."

"Where are you going for the holidays?"

Annie blinked, her blue eyes briefly clouded before she turned to pick up the bucket. "I'm not going anywhere. I'll be here."

Not wanting to intrude, Shea turned her attention back to the pair of goats. She'd actually surprised herself by asking an impertinent question. Must be the McAllisters' influence. "How many animals do you have on the premises?"

"Right now we have twenty-three bison, six sows, a pair of potbellied pigs, eight donkeys, at least three dozen goats and more than two hundred horses. The chickens we keep for eggs."

"I had no idea there were so many residents."

"It varies. Right now, we're really overcrowded, more than even the time of year can account for. But it's cyclical." Annie grinned. "Sorry you volunteered?"

"No, I just don't know how you keep up. The feed bill alone has to be outrageous."

"It is." She wasn't smiling now. Her expression grim, she carried the bucket to a spigot and started filling it with water. "We've always held on by a thread, relying on the charity of a few foundations and the ranchers in the area. This economy has made everything worse. It about killed me but I had to refuse three bison earlier this week."

Shea started to question their fate but decided she didn't want to know. "How many people does it take to keep Safe Haven running?"

"Hard to say…the place manages to run no matter what, but we're never fully staffed. I figure five full-timers would be optimal. As it stands, we make do with six permanent part-time volunteers and myself. I live here, so that works out." Annie exchanged the full bucket for an empty one, then carried the water to large plastic bins plugged into an electrical box. "God, we use so much electricity in the winter just to keep the water from freezing." She motioned with her chin. "Plus the heat lamps. Then there's more hay and feed to buy because there's no grass for grazing."

"I read on your website that you try to find homes for the animals."

"We had two adoptions yesterday, so that was awesome. The holidays are tricky." Annie shook her head. "Kids beg their parents to get them pets for Christmas. They give in, discover it's too costly or too much responsibility, and we end up taking the animal back by mid-January. I try to vet anyone interested but you never know. You mind turning off the water?"

"Sure." Shea hurried over to shut off the spigot, then picked up the bucket. It was far heavier than she'd anticipated, and she grunted with the effort it took to clear the ground.

Annie was kind enough to hide her smile. "I wish more

men would get their butts out here and volunteer. Some of this work is plain brutal on the back, especially if you're not used to physical labor." She took the bucket from Shea and emptied the water into another bin. "Jesse's really good about helping out but I hate to bother him…he has enough on his plate."

Good thing Shea no longer held the bucket or she would've dropped it. "Jesse McAllister volunteers here?"

"Not exactly. He flies for shelters across the state and a few in Wyoming, but he's good enough to do some pickups and drop-offs for us when the route's on his way. We could never afford to chip in for fuel and plane maintenance like the better-funded shelters do."

"But I thought…" She shook her head, totally confused. Jesse worked at the Sundance. It wasn't just an assumption on her part. They'd talked…just yesterday…he'd told her that himself… Oh, God, she didn't know what he'd told her versus what she'd heard. He'd had her so messed up. "He hadn't mentioned he was a pilot."

"He learned to fly in the air force."

"Oh." Shea cleared her throat.

"It's not a secret." Annie walked toward the stall where Angel had finished nursing, and let the goat out. Then she released Kiki from the harness while cooing to her about what a good mother she was. Kiki responded by using her nose to knock the empty metal bowl off the stump. "You've had enough, you little piggy. Now go on."

"Do you have instructions written down?" Shea asked, watching the woman shoo the goat into the general population and wondering how she was ever going to keep all this straight. It didn't help that her thoughts kept drifting to Jesse. One thing for certain, she'd have to stay away from him if she kept losing her concentration.

Annie smiled. "I can do that, and you know I'm going to be around."

"Will Jesse?" Shea groaned when she realized the words had actually tumbled into the ether. "I mean, it doesn't matter if he is or not, so I'm not sure why I asked."

"Hey, I don't blame you." Annie grinned a little wickedly. "He's hot. And smart. And loves animals. What's not to like?"

"You misunderstood. I'm rather hoping he isn't around."

"Huh." Annie studied her a moment and then shrugged. "He seems like a terrific guy. I only met him a little over a year ago after he got out of the service."

"No, he's great. I didn't mean to imply otherwise. I got the dates mixed up and arrived a day early so he took me on a trail ride yesterday."

"Nice." Her brows rose. "I would've expected Trace to be the one who threw out the welcome mat. Jesse's usually so quiet. Quite a few women around here would give their souls to go out with him."

And you? The words teetered on Shea's lips but this time she managed to keep it to herself.

Annie opened a metal trash can, dipped in a scoop and scattered feed for the chickens. "Not me, though. Another time, another place, and oh, yeah," she said, a touch of wistfulness in her voice, unmistakable even to Shea. "I'm not looking for a relationship. This place keeps me busy enough." She replaced the lid. "But good to know Jesse is circulating. I should talk him and some of the other guys into a bachelor auction for a fundraiser. That would keep this place in grain and feed for the winter. Don't say anything to him. We might not see him again."

She didn't have to tell Shea twice. She couldn't imagine Jesse's reaction to being auctioned off like a prize bull in front of a room full of salivating women.

"So where did you go on your ride?" Annie asked. "Toward Mount Edith?"

"I don't recall that name. We stayed in the foothills, I think, but it was beautiful. I wish I was a better rider."

"You can practice all you want here. It's not a requirement, but the permanent volunteers take turns exercising the horses. You're welcome to climb into a saddle anytime."

"Thanks." She followed Annie outside. The sky had lightened up considerably. Behind them the sun was rising over the distant rolling hills and she could see a fenced-in area where horses gathered in small groups. Closer to the barn there were more goats. "How many acres belong to Safe Haven?"

"Almost two hundred, all donated." She indicated a small cabin Shea hadn't noticed before. "There's coffee inside. I'm ready for a cup. How about you?"

"Definitely."

They took the short walk in silence, while Shea mentally debated if another question about Jesse would be inappropriate. It wasn't anything personal so she didn't see the harm. "What exactly does Jesse do for the shelters?"

"He flies rescue flights for injured animals, especially if time is critical or they're found in the mountains and it's too difficult to get to them. He also transports animals to no-kill shelters and foster homes. Or say someone in Wyoming sees a picture of a potbellied pig online from a Montana shelter, Jesse would fly the pig to a Wyoming shelter that would facilitate the adoption. He's in demand because he can fly both a Cessna and helicopters. He even has access to an old cargo plane for the big animals."

"Does he own them?"

"No. That would cost a small fortune. The bigger shelters contribute to fuel and maintenance, and there's a small airfield not too far from the Sundance that donates the hangar space. Jesse does the upkeep and the flying." She stopped at the door and scraped the bottom of her boots on a thick bristly rug.

Shea followed suit and immediately smelled the coffee

as she crossed the threshold. The place was tiny. Basically it was one room with wooden floors and a loft. What passed for the kitchen appeared to be a short counter hosting a microwave and a coffeemaker that flanked a sink. A pair of worn tan leather recliners shared a narrow oak table that was stacked with books. Behind it was a goose-neck floor lamp, and a fire blazed in the wood-burning stove, keeping the room quite toasty.

"In case you couldn't tell, this is where I live," Annie said, indicating the personal items scattered around. "I'm not usually this messy but I'll be damned if I could find the backup can of coffee I swore I bought last week."

Shea accepted the chipped blue mug of coffee Annie passed her, then shook her head to the small pitcher of milk. "I can pick some up in town on the way to the Sundance."

Annie hesitated. "I haven't checked under my bed yet," she said, her gaze going to the stairs leading to the loft.

"It's not like it'll go bad."

"No..." The reluctance was still there.

Shea took her first sip of the sadly weak brew and instantly understood. "Consider it my donation."

A smile lit Annie's face and she clinked Shea's mug with hers. "I won't turn it down."

Ridiculously pleased that she could do something that mattered to this woman, Shea drank her coffee. First Rachel, then Jamie and now Annie—it was crazy, but these women somehow seemed like friends. Using the term loosely, of course, because Shea didn't easily forge relationships with anyone much less people she'd just met.

Mahler's Adagietto suddenly jolted her out of her reverie. It took a moment to realize the classical music was coming from Annie's cell phone. She dug it out of her jeans pocket, her brows dipping into a frown as she answered the call.

"Yeah, Russell, what's up?" Annie paused and listened.

"Is he injured?" she asked, and Shea's heart sunk to her stomach. "Okay, so you'll be here in about an hour?" Annie's gaze went to the plain white wall clock. "No problem, really, it's okay," she said, disconnected the call and sighed heavily. "I lied. We have a problem."

6

SHEA HAD ALWAYS considered the notion of love at first sight silly. Her parents were proof the idea held no merit. But the minute she saw Caleb, the beautiful two-year-old roan being led by Annie from the horse trailer, Shea experienced a wash of emotion for which she had no words. Holding her breath she stared at the magnificent creature of her childhood dreams. The long pinkish-blond mane was tangled and his light chestnut body too lean, but he was still a superb horse.

She felt as if she were ten years old again, kneeling at her bed on Christmas Eve, palms pressed together, head bowed, praying with all her might she would awake to find a miracle on her front lawn.

"Easy, boy," Annie whispered when the horse's hooves hit the ground and he danced restlessly to the left.

"You need help getting him to the stables?" Russell came around from the front of the truck with a rope in his hands. He was a friend of Annie's who worked for the government in controlling the mustang population. It was pure luck that he'd found Caleb, who'd been abandoned.

"No, I'm good. I've already called Doc Yardley for an evaluation. He should be here within the hour."

"I hated springing this on you, Annie." The stocky man

in his mid-forties raked a hand through his hair. "Shitty time of year, I know."

"You've bailed me out plenty of times. Don't worry about it. Go home. Get back to Butte and be with your wife and kids."

"He was a little skittish when I loaded him. Don't know when he ate last so I gave him what little feed I had in the truck. Let me take him while you sign the paperwork."

Annie's gaze never wavered from Caleb as she backed up, bringing him with her. "You have it ready?"

"Right here." He pulled it out of his back pocket. "Hopefully I can get you some reimbursement for his upkeep 'til we move him."

As if he understood what was being said, Caleb suddenly planted his forelegs and refused to budge. Sides heaving, his velvet nostrils fluttering in distress, he nickered low and deep.

"What spooked him?" Annie murmured.

"I don't know." Russell stood at the ready.

"May I try?" Shea asked.

Annie darted her an astonished look. "Leading him?"

"Yes."

"I'm not sure that's a good idea… Careful," Annie said sternly when Shea moved to stroke his neck.

Caleb seemed to relax and turned his head toward Shea, his ears pricked forward with curiosity.

"You want to come with me, you sweet boy?" She slowly reached for the lead.

Annie was hesitant to release it, which Shea totally understood. She sent her a brief beseeching look, anyway. But the deal wasn't sealed until Caleb took a calm step toward Shea.

Her heart nearly pounding through her chest, she felt the lead being pressed into her hand and she gingerly moved in the direction of the stables. "You're safe now, sweetie," she whispered to him, aware that Annie was shadowing her closely. "I've got you."

Shea understood Annie's concern, though she herself wasn't worried one bit. Of all the places she could've chosen to spend Christmas, this was why she'd come here. Who knew Montana was the place she'd finally feel at home?

JESSE WAS WORKING late in the barn when he saw headlights turn down the driveway. He hoped it was Shea because if it wasn't her, he'd end up calling Annie to see what the hell was going on. And man, he did not want to get involved, but Shea should've been back by now.

It wasn't just him. Rachel was worried, too. When she'd called him inside for dinner an hour ago, he'd thought she might've heard from their guest. Failing that, he figured he could count on his sister to make the call. But she hadn't, and he'd refused to say a word, and now that the sun had been down for two hours, it was colder than shit and if that wasn't Shea's car, then he'd have to…

He didn't know what he'd do because he had no business thinking about her at all. Yesterday it had been crystal clear to him that she was someone he needed to stay away from. She was…complicated. So what was he doing? Why was he worried about her? She was a big girl. Maybe subconsciously he was looking for a distraction. But that wasn't like him.

The motion detector lights he'd put up after the horse trailer was stolen a few months earlier, flooded the driveway and glinted off her silver rental as it got closer to the stables. He was more relieved than he had a right to be, he wouldn't deny it…certainly not to himself. Now he couldn't decide if he should walk out to meet her or go back into the barn, act as if it was just a fluke that he'd been standing in the entryway.

Muttering a curse, he tossed the rag he'd been using to clean out a distributor cap and grabbed his hat off the workbench. He settled the Stetson on his head, then tugged down the brim to keep the floodlight's glare out of his eyes.

Apparently Shea hadn't seen him yet. She slipped out of the SUV, went around to the back and lifted the hatch.

"You need help carrying anything?" he asked.

She jumped, her hand going to her throat. "You startled me."

"Yeah, I see that. Sorry."

Her hair was a wild mess, as if she'd been riding in the wind, her cheeks flushed pink and her eyes alive with excitement. "I'm glad you're here. I have a question for you." She reached into the back of the SUV, still talking. "I bought this for Caleb and I want to make sure it's all right to stay in the car overnight."

Jesse's attention snagged on the curve of her nicely rounded backside and it took him a second to process what she'd said.

"Caleb?" So she'd met someone. He didn't recognize the name. Had to be a fellow volunteer. Well, good for her, he thought grimly.

"Yes." She backed up, each arm wrapped around large cans of Colombian coffee.

He frowned, not sure what she expected him to say. "What is it, a Christmas present?"

"What?" She stared at him as if he were the one being weird. Then she glanced at the cans in her arms and laughed. "No, not the coffee…that." She managed to point inside the SUV but almost dropped everything.

He caught one of the cans, drawing close enough to her to get a whiff of vanilla-scented skin under the familiar smell of hay.

"Thanks," she said. "I should've put these in the backseat. Mind opening the door for me?"

"Sure," he said and watched her grab yet another can of coffee. He tilted his head to the side to see what else she'd bought and caught a glimpse of a fourth can, along with stacks of fifty-pound bags of corn and oats. Jesse smiled. "Caleb's a horse."

She nodded, her eyes shining. "A gorgeous strawberry roan. He's only two years old and so beautiful and sweet-tempered. You have to see him, Jesse. You just have to. I can't imagine how someone could've abandoned him."

The temptation to touch her soft smiling lips caught him off guard and he moved back a step. "The coffee isn't for him, I hope."

Shea laughed, hugging the cans to her breast. "These are for Annie. She's down to her last dregs so I thought I'd surprise her." Her expression sobered. "Safe Haven operates on such a shoestring I think she'd use her last dollar on the animals before she'd buy anything for herself."

"You're right about that." He scooped up the last can and went to open the back door. "Did you wipe the Food Mart out of coffee?"

"Almost. I left one on the shelf out of guilt when I heard they can't restock for two days." She waited until he'd stowed the can he held, then handed him the other two. "I hope I don't offend her by bringing these."

"Nah, when it comes to the shelter, Annie has no pride. She'll take all the help she can get. That includes plying the volunteers with coffee."

"Oh, shoot." She wrinkled her nose. "I should've picked up cream and sugar for the others." She didn't move, just stared into space, trapping him against the open car door and giving him no room to maneuver. "I leave too early to stop in town tomorrow."

This wasn't good—her standing so close and the light from the stables shining in her face. Her skin, her lips…she looked so soft it made him itch to touch her. "My mom keeps a hefty supply of sugar on hand. She can help you there. Don't know about the cream."

"Oh, that would be great, then I can replace it."

He waited for her to move. Finally, he touched the back of her arm.

"Sorry, sorry." She scooted back, far back. Shoving the tousled hair away from her face, she gave him a sheepish smile as he walked around to the rear of the SUV.

"You had a question about the feed?"

"Will these bags be all right left out here? I know the temperature will drop below freezing tonight."

"They'll be fine," he said carefully, not wanting to make her feel like an idiot by pointing out the obvious. Feed was always kept outside. What concerned him was that Annie had taken in another horse. He knew she had little money left to feed the animals she currently housed and had made the painful decision to refuse new rescues until she obtained more funding. The other thing was, the oats and corn wouldn't go far and hay was cheaper. "Did Annie ask you to pick up those bags?"

"No. It was a last-minute impulse when I stopped in town. I wanted it to be a treat for Caleb."

Jesse chuckled. "I see."

Her chin went up defensively. "Mr. Jorgensen at the feed and hardware store explained that Annie needs more hay—the alfalfa kind—so I placed an order. He thinks he can have it delivered in a couple days."

"You're paying for that?"

"Yes, I already wrote him a check." Her defensiveness rose. "Safe Haven accepts donations."

"Hey, I'm not criticizing. Annie's going to be thrilled." So was Jorgensen. Business had been bad for everyone the past few years. Jesse wished the Sundance could contribute more hay to Safe Haven, but they'd already done what they could for the season. He liked that Shea had stepped in. Somehow her generosity didn't surprise him.

"I have the money," Shea said, shrugging, then closing the back hatch. "That's not a problem. As long as the weather cooperates, the delivery should come before Christmas Eve."

He looked up at the dark sky—lots of stars, a few clouds. A light snow was forecasted for tomorrow night, but not enough to worry about. "It's real nice what you're doing. Times have been tough for Safe Haven. If Annie needs help unloading, Trace and I will drive out there."

She gave him a long thoughtful look. "I heard you do a lot for them."

"Nah, not that much." He wondered what Annie had said about him. He knew people talked since he'd returned home. They all had an opinion about why he wasn't the same old Jesse, though Annie didn't strike him as the type to gossip. He nudged his chin toward the house. "We had fried chicken and mashed potatoes tonight. Rachel's keeping a plate warm for you."

Shea's expression fell. "I wish she wouldn't do that."

"Feed you?" He smiled when she carelessly shoved her hair away from her face and rolled her eyes. "What kind of reputation will the Sundance have if we starve our guests?"

"I'm sure you have a stellar reputation. Your whole family is wonderful," she said, then glanced away. "Jeez, I say I don't want to be a bother and then I keep you out here in the cold."

"Such a hardship."

She slid him a hesitant look, saw he was teasing and a small smile tugged at her lips.

Dammit, he had the sudden urge to kiss that shy, sexy mouth. "Come on, I'll walk you to the house."

"You don't have to—" They'd already moved in that direction, but she stopped, eyes wide, lips parted in awe. "That Christmas tree, it's beautiful."

Jesse followed her gaze to the ten-foot pine he'd helped Rachel put up in the foyer. White lights glittered from the branches, five hundred of the tiny suckers—he happened to know because he'd bitched about having to string them. But looking at Shea's unadulterated delight made the chore worth it.

"It's huge and so perfect. I've never seen one like it before." She swung her gaze toward him. "That couldn't have been there last night." She paused. "Was it?"

"That would've been pretty hard to miss."

"Trust me, I can overlook an elephant in the middle... Never mind."

"I cut it down this morning."

"You?"

"Yes, me. I'm not as scrawny as I look."

"I didn't mean—" The instant she saw he was teasing she smiled, something she didn't do nearly enough. Not a real smile like this one that showed off her straight white teeth, or the pretty shape of her pink lips. She turned back to the tree, her face lit as if she were a kid who'd been visited by Santa. "Where did you find it?"

"Not far from the trail we took yesterday. It's McAllister land so it's legal."

"I have mixed feelings about cutting down something so glorious." She sighed. "I'm a hypocrite. I love being able to see it every night."

"If we don't thin out the forest, nature will. We've had some bad lightning strikes that have taken down acres of trees. Had a wildfire this past August that wiped out half a hill of spruce and pine."

She stopped a few feet from the porch, hands shoved deep into the pockets of her jacket, and just stared at the tree even though she'd started to shiver. "I like the red ribbons and candy canes."

"We used up the ornaments on the trees in the den and living room. Mom and Rachel tend to get carried away this time of year."

"Were the other trees up last night?"

"Have been since the day after Thanksgiving."

"Oh, I'd love to see them sometime." She shivered and hunched her shoulders. "If that would be all right."

"Come on before you freeze. The tree looks just as pretty inside as it does out here." He took her by the elbow and gently urged her toward the steps before he did something stupid like wrap his arms around her.

"I'm kind of hoping it snows for Christmas," she said, pulling a hand out of her pocket to hold the railing.

"We're supposed to get some tomorrow night. Not much, only three or four inches."

"That sounds like a lot."

"You have four-wheel drive." He glanced over his shoulder toward her car. "You'll be okay." Something unpleasant occurred to him and he stopped in front of the door. "You do know how to drive in snow?"

She nibbled at her lower lip. "Guess I'll find out."

"I hope you're kidding."

"The roads will be plowed, right?"

He studied her face. She had to be pulling his leg. Nobody came to Montana in the middle of winter unable to drive in snow. Except, she was beginning to look more uncertain by the second. *Shit.* "I'll drive you tomorrow."

"Absolutely not." She pulled away and grabbed the doorknob. "But thanks, anyway." She hesitated. "Should I ring the doorbell?"

He pushed open the door, tension coiling in his gut. He didn't want to be the bad guy and bully her into accepting a ride. He'd mention something to Rachel and let her talk to Shea. This was her doing after all. *Her* guest.

Once they entered the foyer and were met with a wave of warmth from the fireplace, he gave reasoning with her another shot. "At least plan to get back before dark so we don't have to send out a search party."

"I can do that."

Her gaze was glued to the tree. Anyone would think she'd never seen one before. "Christmas must be your favorite time of year."

"Not really," she said. "You?"

"It was when I was a kid." A lot had happened since then—his father's death, the recession, going to war. "Rachel still gets excited." He pulled off his gloves. "Don't tell her Santa isn't real. It would crush her."

Shea blinked and looked at him with a guileless expression. "Why would I do that? Santa is real."

Jesse saw the glint of humor in her eyes and something inside him shifted. Something that had been dormant a long time. Okay, so maybe there was a little magic in the season. "What did you say you did for a living again?"

She sniffed, lifting her chin, exposing the slender column of her throat. "Excuse me, but even nerds can have senses of humor."

His gaze drifted to her top button right at the hollow of her throat. That was another thing about winter that sucked. Too many clothes. "*Nerd* was not what came to mind." He raised his eyes and caught the faint blush that stole across her cheeks. "How about something hot to drink? Coffee, chocolate, brandy? I could use something."

"There you are." Rachel came from the dining room, a dish towel slung over her shoulder. "I was beginning to worry," she said to Shea.

"I'm sorry. I stopped in town."

"No problem. Dinner's in the oven whenever you're ready." Rachel's smile faded as she looked at Jesse. "I could've used your help in the kitchen. You know Hilda's off for two weeks. That doesn't make me the maid around here."

Jesse snorted. "Yeah, because I've been twiddling my thumbs all day." He glanced pointedly at the tree, then slid Shea a private wink. Hard to tell if she understood that Rachel was only messing with him. "Where's Trace? I'd like to see him walking around in an apron for a change."

"I heard that." Trace's voice came from the den, a second before the distinct clack of billiard balls bouncing off one another echoed through the first floor.

"Rachel, Shea…" It was Jamie's voice rising above the sound of male laughter. "I need backup in here."

"You play pool?" Jesse asked Shea.

She shook her head and was already moving toward the staircase. "Rachel, thanks for keeping dinner for me…it's so nice of you, but I wish you hadn't gone to the trouble." Her arms were pressed against her body as if she were trying to make herself smaller. "I've already eaten in town. But again, I appreciate your concern." She swept a glance toward Jesse, then took a final look at the tree. "It was a long day. I think I'll crawl into bed."

They watched her hurry up the stairs and disappear.

"Hmm, a woman around here who doesn't want to be any trouble," Jesse murmured. "Imagine that."

"Yeah, you're hilarious." Rachel studied the empty landing at the top of the stairs. "Is she okay?"

"I think so."

"Weren't you guys talking for a while?"

He nodded, his mind still trying to process what had just happened. She'd been warming up to him in the last few minutes.

"You didn't say anything boneheaded, did you?"

Giving his sister a dry look, Jesse blew out a stream of air. Without another word, he turned around and left through the front door and headed for the solitude of the barn. Thinking about Shea was getting him in deeper and deeper. Hell, he knew better. He should've trusted his first instinct to keep as far away from her as possible.

She might seem timid and fragile, like the animals he rescued, but she was a grown woman with her own mind. She didn't need him.

7

"WHAT'S ALL THIS?" Dressed in the same battered parka as yesterday, her blond hair crammed under a woolen cap, Annie stopped in the middle of scooping grain when she saw Shea approach. She dropped the cut-out plastic milk jug she used as a scoop and moved toward Shea. "You're an angel," Annie said, relieving her of one of the cans of coffee. "Seriously, a damn angel."

Shea chuckled. "I have another can in the car. Some other things, too, that I'll need help unloading. Take a look and tell me if I should move the car closer."

Annie stashed the coffee on a railing, and with her longer legs hurried ahead of Shea toward the SUV. She stared at the bags of oats and corn, not looking nearly as pleased as Shea had hoped.

"I bought the wrong thing," Shea said, trying to hide her disappointment. This was her second letdown of the day and it was only seven-fifteen. She'd come downstairs to find that Jesse had been called away an hour earlier to fly a rescue mission.

"No, not at all." Annie's mouth curved in a gentle smile. "It's just that...this feed probably won't go as far as you're expecting."

"Oh. No, I get that. This is just kind of a special treat for Caleb and the sick mares." She hadn't planned on blabbing about the hay delivery yet. It would've been fun to keep it a surprise, but she wanted to relieve Annie's concerns. "Mr. Jorgensen from the hardware store is arranging for a truck-load of hay in a couple days."

"A truckload?" Annie frowned. "How did you manage that?"

"Nothing magical." Shea shrugged. "I wrote him a check."

"Hay isn't cheap, especially this time of year."

"It's okay, Annie. I wouldn't have done it if I didn't have the money." She almost touched the other woman's arm. A totally natural display of comfort or affection, she supposed, just not for her.

Annie covered her mouth with her hand, her eyes moist. Except her hand was gloved and she jerked it away, sniffed and said, "Ew."

They both laughed.

"You're getting a hug," Annie said. "Too bad about my gloves." She threw her arms around Shea before she could utter a word, and amazingly, it was okay. She didn't get all squeamish like she normally did when someone got touchy-feely.

Still, Shea pulled back first. "Jesse said he and Trace would come help unload if you need them."

"He knew about you doing this?"

"After the fact."

Amusement gleamed in Annie's eyes. "Sounds like you might be getting to Jesse."

"What?"

"I swear, he's said more to you in the short time you've been here than he has to anyone in a month."

"That can't be true," Shea said, feeling the heat crawl up her neck. Luckily, she heard a vehicle turn into the lot.

Molly and Hank, the other new volunteers, pulled up in Hank's late-model Ford pickup and parked closer to the barn. They were a middle-aged couple from Billings. At least Shea assumed they were a couple…she really wasn't sure. They seemed nice, and eager to learn. That's all she knew about them. Every free moment yesterday she'd spent with Caleb.

Annie waved them over. "Good, we have help carrying these bags." Her lips pursed, she turned back to Shea as they waited for the couple. "I wasn't giving you a hard time about Jesse. If anything I'm glad he's showing signs of coming back to life."

Shea still felt uncomfortable over how much she'd talked about Jesse yesterday, but she couldn't exactly tell Annie to stop. It didn't help that she was a little flabbergasted at what Annie'd actually said. "What do you mean?"

"I didn't know him before he went to Afghanistan, but the buzz around town is that he's changed. He's always been a quiet kind of guy. I've never thought much of it but you hear people who've known him his whole life talk and…" She shrugged and quickly switched her attention to Molly and Hank, who were walking toward them. "Obviously I've lived here too long," Annie muttered with a self-deprecating frown. "Gossiping like an old lady. God help me."

The volunteers who Shea, Molly and Hank were replacing started arriving for their last day before the holidays. They all pitched in to carry the bags of feed, make coffee and cut up the homemade banana bread that Molly had brought. Shea tried to be patient and not seem rude through the small talk and early chores, but she would have much rather been spending time with Caleb. She'd always found the company of animals soothing, but there was something special about the roan.

However, even Caleb wasn't enough to keep her thoughts from Jesse and what she'd just learned about him. She wondered what would've happened last night if Rachel hadn't shown up, or if the others hadn't been playing pool in the next room. Would they have continued to talk? Maybe even sat down at the table together? It hadn't occurred to her until she'd been lying in bed that when they were alone she was completely comfortable with him.

Well, not completely...he did tend to make her heart beat a little faster than normal. And she was starting to become a bit obsessive about the cleft in his chin. And the way his smile always started off real slow, like he had a secret he couldn't share.

It wasn't until close to noon that Shea had a chance to breathe without feeling guilty. The new volunteers were still learning the daily routines and she was starting to feel the stiffness of yesterday's physical labor. When Annie suggested she take a break and give Caleb some oats, Shea didn't object.

She scooped a generous portion into a plastic pail and carried it to his stall. For today, he was still getting preferential treatment and being kept in the stable with the sick mares even though Doc Yardley had given him a clean bill of health. Tomorrow he would be turned out to pasture with the rest of the horses. She hated the idea.

For one thing, today the sky wasn't as clear and blue. The clouds weren't threatening, but it was overcast, the sun only intermittently breaking through, which meant the air was colder than yesterday.

"Hi, sweetie."

At the sound of her voice, Caleb lifted his head, saw it was her and lowered his muzzle with his ears forward.

Shea laughed. "Is that for me or do you smell these oats?" She faced him nose-to-muzzle and blew gently into his nostrils just as Annie had taught her. He promptly responded by lowering his head, and Shea grinned with delight at the gelding's open display of friendship.

"Look what I have for you." His attention had already turned to the pail and she had to move quickly before he ended up sticking his muzzle too far in.

She gave him his oats, felt guilty that she'd brought none for the mares on either side of him, though she hadn't gotten permission to feed them. They'd both come to the shelter sick last week and had only just recovered.

While Caleb ate, she went to the back of the stable to check on Maisy, an older bay mare who was being kept in isolation and treated for a parasitic infection. Her previous owners had thrown up their hands when the vet bills mounted. Safe Haven couldn't afford the poor horse's care, either, and if Shea let it, thinking about the myriad problems and expense of so many of the animals that had been abandoned, neglected or injured could really depress her.

Instead, she focused on the good things the sanctuary was doing for their wards. Tomorrow Annie was going to review the individualized diets they provided, and in the evenings Shea was going to work on a computer program that would simplify the files and records to avoid mistakes by the volunteers.

She heard Caleb trying to get her attention with his quiet nicker. "You ate too fast, mister," she said, moving toward his stall. He looked at her with his large soft brown eyes and she sighed. "No, I can't give you any more. Maybe later. But I do have another surprise. Annie says I can exercise you this afternoon. How would you like that?"

Shea squeezed a section of his beautiful strawberry mane between her thumb and forefinger, and rubbed the strands together, trying to mimic how another horse would groom him with its teeth. Another friendly overture Annie had shown her. He liked that a lot. Though not so much when she worked her fingers up and down his tangled mane. Sad how his owner had neglected his grooming.

According to Russell, who knew the man, he wasn't a bad person, simply another victim of the struggling economy. She understood...sort of. The upside was that Russell knew enough about Caleb that Annie felt comfortable allowing Shea to ride him.

She heard voices coming from outside the stables and her gaze went to her watch, her insides clenching because she knew it was time for shots. It was a good thing, relieving the colic horses of pain, but even thinking about needles gave her the willies. Hank was diabetic. He had no problem administering the shots. Besides, he had two horses of his own at home.

"He is a handsome fella," Hank said, stopping to admire Caleb. Jim, the volunteer who was taking off for the holidays, was with him. "You thinking about adopting him?"

"Me?" Shea blinked. "I live in an apartment in California."

"Too bad. He's sure taken a liking to you." Hank stepped closer, squinting over the rim of his thick glasses. "Good teeth. Plenty of lean muscle. Hasn't been neglected for too long." Hank grunted. "That's the trouble with volunteering in a place like this. You wanna take 'em all home with you."

She wasn't prepared for the surge of jealousy that swelled in her throat. Her reaction was totally inappropriate. Caleb wasn't her horse. And the idea was to find him a home, after all. "Annie said I can exercise him later," she said for no reason.

Jim's smile was kind and knowing. He was a retired schoolteacher who'd been raised on a ranch. "After you ride him, I'll have to remove his hind shoes before we turn him out to pasture with the others." Jim glanced outside. "I'd like to do it by two. I'm leaving a little early to beat the snow."

"Why remove his shoes?" she asked, alarmed, then vaguely considered that she should've been more concerned about the weather.

"They kick out at each other even when they're just playing. We don't need any of them getting hurt."

It struck Shea that since Caleb was being let out to pasture he didn't need exercising. Annie was simply being nice. And if Shea wanted to be a nice person, she shouldn't hold up Jim from his duties just so she could ride Caleb.

Apparently she wasn't that nice. It was just that she wanted to ride Caleb so badly....

Both men had already moved to the rear of the stables where the sick horses were kept. She refused to so much as glance back there, not wanting to see the needles come out, but she stopped at the door and, staring at the gray sky, called to Jim. "I'll go find out if I can ride him now."

She didn't wait for an acknowledgment but ran toward the corral, where she saw Annie talking on her cell phone. Shea stood several feet out of earshot, waiting impatiently, and ended up getting roped into helping Molly refill water troughs for the pigs and goats. By the time Annie got off the phone, Jim was finished in the stables and had rounded up the volunteers to cover the stacked bales of hay with tarp.

An hour later, Shea caught up with Annie and obtained her permission. By then everyone seemed worried about the snow. It had already started coming down in Kalispell and the higher elevations, and there was some disagreement among the local forecasters over when it would hit the rest of the state and how many inches to expect. All Shea could think about was riding Caleb.

As soon as she ran into the stables she sensed something was wrong beyond the nagging doubt that she'd be able to saddle a horse unsupervised. The problem was the gate to Caleb's stall—it was wide open. She held her breath as she moved close enough to look inside.

Her beautiful strawberry roan was gone.

"I CAN DO THIS," she pleaded. "Please, Annie, give me an hour." Shea could tell by the tight pull of the woman's mouth that Shea wasn't getting anywhere. "Okay, how about half an hour? I'll ride for fifteen minutes, then turn around and head back to Safe Haven whether I find him or not."

"It could start snowing before then. You could get lost. Caleb will be all right." Annie used the back of her wrist to wipe the sweat from her brow.

A last-minute donation of produce discards from a Butte food chain had been delivered and had to be stored properly. Everyone was hustling to beat the possible storm and Shea knew she was being utterly selfish in badgering the poor woman, but all she could think about was Caleb, cold and hungry with no shelter. She wished she didn't need anyone's blessing. But the only way she could go after him was to borrow a horse. Maybe she was being irrational, maybe Annie was right and Caleb would be fine....

She couldn't let it go. "First flake that hits my face I'll turn around. You said yourself Caleb likely didn't stray far. Chances are I'll find him in a few minutes." Using all her might, Shea dragged a crate marked *bruised apples* toward the barn. She wanted to help, but mostly she could no longer look into Annie's eyes and see the toll her persistence was taking on the poor woman who already had too much on her mind right now.

"Please let me borrow a horse," she said quietly, guilt stabbing deep this time. This was it. She wouldn't ask again. "I promise not to endanger him."

Annie visibly took a deep breath and held up a gloved finger. "First sign it's snowing."

"The very first."

"You follow the fence line, stay on flat land and ride only fifteen minutes, then turn around no matter what."

"No matter what," Shea repeated, her legs suddenly quivering from pent-up nerves.

"Candy Cane knows you, take her. She's gentle but headstrong." The corner of Annie's mouth quirked. "Sound familiar?"

"Thank you, Annie." She'd already started backing up. "I'll be careful."

"You rode with Jesse—that tells me something, or the answer would've been no. Use the tack on the far wall and take your time saddling her. I know you're in a hurry but you don't wanna start off by making her edgy."

"Got it." Shea understood the truth in that and focused on her deep breathing exercise.

Annie started to say something else but someone interrupted her, and Shea took the opportunity to hurry toward the stables. She resisted the impulse to run. Breathe deeply, that's what she had to do. Keep calm.

Before she'd realized she was doing it, she'd begun counting in multiples of three, briefly pausing between each set. Screw it. The habit helped relax her and now wasn't the time to practice alternate therapy.

By the time she'd saddled Candy Cane and they were heading out of the stables, Shea had centered herself. Until she saw the black clouds overhead. The sky looked bad as far as she could see. Half surprised that Annie hadn't shown up to tell her she'd reconsidered, Shea nudged the mare into a gallop headed in the opposite direction from Annie and the rest of the group.

JESSE CURSED HIMSELF for being a fool. He never should've stopped at the Billings recruitment office after dropping off the injured ram. If he hadn't been so damn impulsive he would've missed the snow. How friggin' stupid, he thought, as the second fat flake splattered against the windshield of the Cessna. Not just stupid but irresponsible. This wasn't his plane.

It wasn't so much a safety issue—he'd flown in snow enough times and this baby had the best deicing equipment he'd ever seen—but the principle involved. The questions he'd had could've been handled over the phone. No need for unnecessary risk. He wouldn't make his decision to reenlist until after the holidays, and if he decided to go back in, it wouldn't be through a recruitment center. The bonus they offered for a ten-year re-up would have to make it worth his while.

What annoyed him was that his mind had been as clouded as the black sky overhead—had been since he'd talked to Shea yesterday. He'd been thinking about her too much. Made no sense, since the only thing he knew for sure was that she had a good heart. He would've liked to see Annie's face when she got the coffee and feed. Three hundred pounds of oats and corn were nothing compared to Safe Haven's need. Shea didn't know that, but she cared enough to stop at Jorgensen's and find out how she could make a difference. The hay delivery would be a godsend.

Coming down faster and harder, the snow pelted the Cessna. Later he could finish ripping himself a new one for being a dumbass, for now he gave his full attention to the controls. It'd be another twenty or thirty minutes to the airstrip he used. His truck was parked there or he'd seriously think about putting down at the Sundance. Nice thing about flying in a rural area—few power lines and sufficient places to land a small plane if the need arose.

He surveyed the ground for one of his landmarks before the place was covered in white. A dozen miles back he'd flown over Vernon's fishing cabin. That meant he was now over Safe Haven land. Damn, he hoped Shea had left early. No need worrying. Annie would've seen to it.

A gust of icy wind buffeted the plane. Wet snow slapped the wings.

"Shit."

Man, when the local meteorologists screwed up they really went all out. It wasn't a blizzard but pretty damn close, with no signs of letting up. He grabbed the radio.

"Piedmont Ground, this is Cessna 55512 over Safe Haven, looking for an area weather report."

Waiting for a response from ground control, Jesse rolled a tense shoulder, then darted a look below. He thought he saw something pink. Probably a trick of the muted light. There was nothing out here. Certainly no reason for a person to be roaming around in this weather. He rubbed his right eye and squinted at the object. Too late, he was already passing.

"Cessna 55512, this is Piedmont Ground, repeat your location."

Jesse didn't recognize the voice. Just what he was afraid of. Paul, the guy who owned the airstrip, must be taking time off. Then something clicked. "Piedmont Ground, this is Cessna 55512, is that you, Stanley?"

"Affirmative, Cessna 55512."

Jesus. It was Paul's nephew, and he knew Jesse. Not much small aircraft activity in these parts during winter. But filling in for his uncle was probably the highlight of Stanley's year. He'd stick to formality even if he knew this was his only communication for the day.

"Hold on, Stanley. Back in a minute."

Jesse had to circle around and have another look. It was probably nothing. All he ever saw were cows or wildlife in the winter. But something pinkish might as well be a red flag. Doubt would nag at him if he didn't put his mind at ease. A couple minutes to backtrack wouldn't kill him.

The snow was coming down like a son of a bitch, though, and he'd be lucky to see anything. As he came around, he gently pushed the wheel down and used the elevator control to drop for a better look.

He'd barely decreased altitude when he saw the shape of a person. A small person. A woman. Wearing a pink jacket.

Shea.

What the hell…

His heart thudded. He should've recognized her jacket immediately.

She sat atop a horse, hunched over its neck. He couldn't tell if she was hurt or trying to shield her face from the blowing snow. And then she must've heard the engine because she tilted her head back, her arm thrown across her forehead, as she stared up into the sky.

Jesse didn't bother signaling. Too much snow. She couldn't see him. He only hoped she had sense enough to keep her eyes on the plane. After he landed, she'd have to come to him.

He picked up the radio again. "Piedmont Ground—Stanley? It's Jesse. Making an emergency landing. Plane is fine. I'm fine. I'll be in touch."

8

SHEA COULD BARELY see the plane circling above. Her pulse pounded so loudly in her ears she'd initially thought she'd imagined hearing the engine. Icy white snowflakes kept falling and the wind was so cold it sliced through her jacket. The weather had gone to hell so fast—she'd never experienced anything like this before.

Candy Cane seemed fine, considering. Probably because the snow hadn't yet accumulated to more than a few inches on the ground. That would change quickly, too, she thought, watching the small aircraft begin to descend. Was the pilot landing? But where? Nothing but fields surrounded them, a couple of small hills, the occasional grove of trees.

He couldn't have been looking for her. She'd only left Safe Haven a half hour ago. Not enough time for Annie to alert anyone. Annie expected Shea back at any minute, but she'd gotten so lost once the snow started. She'd tried to head back to Safe Haven. She had.

She couldn't think about that right now. Something could be wrong with the plane. Maybe the pilot was in trouble.

A crazy thought popped into her head. Was it Jesse? No, too big a coincidence. Although he was expected back this afternoon, and how many people would be flying on a day like this if they could avoid it?

She sucked the frigid air into her unsuspecting lungs and winced at the pain. Using her arm to block the snow from flying directly into her face, she tried to keep sight of the plane while it continued to lose altitude. The descent seemed controlled, so maybe nothing was wrong. For all she knew, a landing strip stretched out on the other side of the rise that would eventually cut off her view of the aircraft.

Shea swallowed the lump of fear forming in her throat, dug her heels into the mare's flanks and urged her forward. It was as good a direction as any. She no longer had a clue where Safe Haven was.

God, she'd promised Annie she'd keep Candy Cane safe. And Caleb…she hadn't caught so much as a glimpse of him. He was out here in the freezing cold, too. Her teeth chattering, she pushed every thought out of her mind except for the plane and the pilot. Darkness seemed to be falling as quickly as the temperature. She had to stay focused, keep her gaze alert through the tricky shifting light.

A minute later, the plane disappeared.

AS SOON AS JESSE LANDED, he radioed Stanley, gave him a brief rundown and asked him to call the Sundance. Rachel would get in touch with Annie. Later, after he made sure Shea was safe, Jesse would contact them again.

He dug out his emergency gear, pulled on a parka and prayed like hell she was on her way toward him. A pair of skis and snowshoes were stowed in the back of the Cessna, but he didn't need them yet. He glanced up at the sky. Within a half hour, he would. The unexpected squall was turning into a damn blizzard.

"What the hell is she doing out here?" he muttered, the fear thick in his voice and in his chest.

Leaving on his sunglasses to cut the glare, he trudged in the direction he'd seen her last. Fortunately the wind was coming from behind him. Good for him, not for Shea. The blowing snow would be partially blinding her. His only consolation was that she had to be riding a good horse. Annie would never have let her out here otherwise. Then again, it wasn't like Annie to allow something like this to happen in the first place.

Jesse muttered a few more choice words he seldom used and pressed forward. Maybe he'd been too hasty to dismiss the snowshoes, although they would've slowed him down. He kept pushing himself, his eyes trained on the top of the small hill she'd have to climb to get to him. He knew exactly what time he'd landed but he didn't bother checking his watch now. The passage of time didn't matter. Getting to her did.

Moments later he saw her. God bless that pink jacket. He didn't think she'd spotted him. Hard to tell with her arm hiding her face.

"Shea," he yelled, letting the wind carry his voice.

When she showed no sign of having heard him, he cupped his gloved hands around his mouth and called again. After two more tries, she lowered her arm. Her shoulders suddenly went back and her mouth opened. He thought she might have said something but he couldn't hear her.

For a second he feared she might spook the mare, but she paused, adjusted her grip on the reins and nudged the horse toward him. His breathing labored from trudging through the thickening snow, he waited where he stood.

"Jesse, are you okay?" she asked, then climbed off the mare before he could stop her. They needed to move quickly.

"You all right?" He caught her by the shoulders, studying her flushed face. Icy snow clung to her hair and eyelashes.

She nodded. "I was looking for Caleb. He got away. Did

you see him from up there…?" She started to look over her shoulder but he gave her a gentle shake.

"Listen, we have to find shelter. Now."

"The plane?" She blinked hard against the snow pelting her face.

He hugged her against him, using his body to protect her. "A cabin not far from here. But we have to go now. Let's get you back in the saddle."

"What about you?" She tilted her head back, her teeth chattering violently.

"I'm fine walking."

"But—"

He lowered his head and kissed her. Not the best way to shut her up but he'd acted on instinct. And it worked. He drew back. "Please don't argue."

The wind howled around them. He doubted she'd heard him. She just stared at him with wide eyes. It would be easy to pick her up and put her back in the saddle. And all he wanted was to kiss her again.

She leaned into him and lifted her mouth.

Damn, they had to get out of here.

He pulled her against his chest and kissed her hard, his tongue probing the seam of her lips. She let him inside and tentatively touched her tongue to his. Her shoulders shook beneath his hands.

This was insane. *He* was insane. He broke away. "We have to go now," he mouthed, unable to compete with the shrieking wind.

She nodded, and he helped her into the saddle.

Noticing the cinch was loose, he reached under the mare, and in spite of his bulky gloves, managed to tighten the strap. It pissed him off that he was somewhat disoriented. He'd been too focused on her instead of monitoring where they were in relation to the line shack that he knew straddled the border between Safe Haven and the Hebers' land.

Once he was confident they were headed in the right direction, he took the reins and motioned for Shea to keep her head down. She didn't object but instantly dropped her chin to her chest. His sunglasses helped protect him somewhat but the way the snow slashed sideways, punishing their exposed skin, he knew it was going to be a long trek.

He led the mare toward the plane, intent on stopping to pick up his emergency kit on the way to the shack. Though he'd flown over the place a few times, he hadn't used it in years. He hoped like hell they weren't in for a nasty surprise.

AT FIRST SHEA THOUGHT the small cabin was a hallucination. It didn't seem possible there'd be a building, such as it was, in the middle of nowhere.

It was also possible this whole thing was a dream. Jesse had kissed her. She'd kissed him back. How could that have been real? Could she have made it up in her head?

Jesse led Candy Cane right up to the door and tethered her to a pole that had been stuck in the ground, buried in nearly a foot of snow. She knew he expected her to dismount but she was so numb from the cold that she feared she'd need his help in order to land on her feet. Which wasn't the least bit fair—he had to be exhausted.

Apparently he hadn't expected her to do anything because he reached up and caught her at the waist. "Ready?"

She nodded, unable to utter a word. Her teeth were still chattering too hard, and the uncontrollable shivering hadn't eased up. She felt like such a baby.

He lifted her off the saddle and set her on the ground. Her legs were unbearably weak, hardly more stable than overcooked spaghetti, and if she went down she'd just die.

Without a word, Jesse slid an arm around her. "No point in me going inside first. We have no other choice."

Grateful for his support, she leaned against him. "I'm just glad it's blocking the wind."

He pushed open the unlatched door, and Shea could've sworn she saw a critter run across the wood floor. Or it might have been a trick of the waning light. Either way, she didn't care. As long as there was no biting involved, she was willing to share.

A dank, musty smell permeated the air, and she didn't care about that, either. As they stumbled across the threshold, she saw the place consisted of a single room with no windows. A cot had been shoved into the corner and beside it sat two small benches that looked like the results of a high school woodshop project.

Other objects were scattered about but it was too dim to make them out. Something big and gray sat in the middle of the room and she got excited when she realized it was a potbellied stove.

"Does this thing work?" she asked, optimism warming her insides.

"I hope so." Jesse removed his arm from around her waist and was slowly inching away. "You okay to stand?"

She had been leaning on him quite heavily. The realization surprised her, but more shocking was the sudden need to keep him glued to her side. "Of course, sorry."

"For what?" He rubbed her arm with reassurance and then dug in the large bag he'd taken from the plane.

She heard a soft click before the round glow from a flashlight swept the small room. The light stopped on a lantern hanging on a rough, unfinished wall. She saw the floor was made up of warped wooden planks and made a mental note to be careful how she stepped.

"I was hoping the lantern was still here." He took her

hand and pressed the flashlight against her palm. "Hold this, would you?"

"How did you know— Have you been here before?"

"Many times." He pulled off one of his gloves, and just watching him expose his hand made her shudder deep inside her jacket. "In fact, my brother Cole and I helped Cy Heber put up this shack twelve years ago."

She tried to keep the beam of light ahead of him while he retrieved the lantern. "It seems older."

"May not be the Ritz, but it's served its purpose more than once."

"I'm not complaining," she said, unable to stop shivering. Nice to be out of the snow but it seemed just as cold inside as outside. "Should I close the door?"

"Let's see if we can air the place out a little." He stopped fidgeting with the lantern, looked over at her and then went back to rooting inside the bag.

He pulled out something big and silvery and draped it around her shoulders, gathering the ends together under her chin. She'd lowered her arms to her side, making the flashlight useless.

"What is this?"

"A blizzard blanket. It helps conserve your body heat."

She couldn't see his face in the murky light but she could feel his breath, warm and moist, dancing across her cheekbones. "What about you?"

"I want to get this lantern lit and a fire started." He brushed his bare thumb along her jaw.

Even though she couldn't see, she was pretty sure his touch to her face was deliberate. Was he thinking about the kiss? Would he say something about it? She kind of hoped he didn't. Still, she liked having him close, wanted him closer. She tried to move her feet, but that didn't work out so well.

"We're going to be okay here," he said quietly, and there

was the slightly rough pad of his thumb again, stroking her jaw, making her want to sag against him. She was exhausted, that's all. "You understand?"

"What about Caleb and Candy Cane?" She saw a flash of white teeth.

"Candy Cane?"

"I didn't name her."

He made sure she had a grip on the blanket before he withdrew his hands. "They'll be fine."

"Please don't lie to me."

"Shine the flashlight over here." He picked up the lantern. "You think people bring their horses and cattle inside when it snows?"

"You don't have to be condescending."

He pulled matches out of his bag of tricks and lit the lantern. The flickering glow caught his faint smile. "You accused me of being a liar." He shrugged. "So we're even."

"I didn't say you— Okay, I sort of did, but I didn't mean it." Sighing, she pushed the hair away from her frozen face, and glanced around the room again now that they had some light.

Logs were stacked on the other side of the stove, so that gave her hope they'd have some heat soon. Closer to her an open cardboard box bulged with kindling and crumpled newspaper. By the far wall was a kettle and an iron frying pan sitting on an overturned metal bucket. Canned goods had been stored in an old corner bookshelf. God only knew how long they'd been sitting there. She wasn't that hungry yet.

Her gaze went back to Jesse. "What can I do to help?" *That won't embarrass me,* she nearly added. She never felt more useless than in a situation like this.

He crouched in front of the stove, opened the small door and used the illumination of the lantern to peer inside. "Find a decent place to sit while I get a fire going. You can use the flashlight."

Either she was getting used to the musty odor, or leaving the door open had worked. She peeked outside to check on Candy. The mare snorted steam but seemed sufficiently content to not have snow blowing in her face. That didn't stop Shea from worrying. Caleb was still out there with no shelter at all.

"Shea, I promise you the horses are fine."

She turned around and watched him arrange the logs inside the stove. "How can you make that promise?"

"We have herds of wild mustangs living in the mountains who survive one winter after another, including their young."

All right, he had a point—one she hadn't considered. "Caleb is domesticated."

"And probably smarter than half the people we know."

She smiled. Another valid point. No doubt the horse was savvier than herself, damn her IQ. She pulled the metallic blanket more snugly around her shoulders and swallowed hard. "I really messed up," she said, mortified when her voice broke.

Jesse's head jerked up. "Hey."

She moved into the shadows so he couldn't see her watery eyes. No tears had fallen yet, and she blinked rapidly to keep them at bay. "Annie must be terrified. If she sends anyone out to look for me in this storm, I'll never forgive—"

"I had someone call her. She knows you're with me." He struck a match and lit the fire. Wisps of dark smoke seeped from the metal pipe that poked through the ceiling.

"How?" There couldn't be cell service out here.

"I radioed when we stopped at the Cessna. Annie and my family have been notified that we're lying low." Rising, he waved off the smoke and inspected the pipe.

"Thank God." She breathed in too deeply and it hurt her chest. Tears still burned at the back of her eyes. She had to get control of herself. They were safe, and Annie and the McAllisters didn't have to worry.

He used the heel of his hand to give the stovepipe a couple of whacks. She heard something break loose inside, then some other rattling noise. Probably an animal. She didn't ask…she didn't want to know. The smoke had stopped leaking. That was good enough for her.

"Close the door if you want," he said, returning to poke at the meager flames.

Her relief that he'd been too preoccupied to notice her almost lose it dissolved when she saw that he was studying her as intently as he was the struggling fire.

Averting her eyes, she silently cleared her throat. "I'm willing to leave it open for a while longer if you think it would help."

"It'll get warmer faster with the door closed."

She had the benefit of the blanket, he didn't. After a final peek at the mare, Shea shut the door. "This is really helping," she said, letting the blanket slide off her shoulders. "You should use it now."

He stood abruptly and stopped her from passing it to him. "No, keep it around you until I have the fire going better. Don't lose heat now."

"What about you?"

"Hey, I'm the hero of the day. Let me enjoy my fame for another hour."

"The hero?"

"Damn right. Rescued a damsel in distress, didn't I?"

"I thought this looked more like a cape than a blanket." God, she'd made a joke of sorts. What had gotten into her?

His mouth curved in a small smile as he gently arranged the blanket so that it covered her shoulders and most of her neck. The whole time he faced her, tugging the ends together and catching her off guard. She stumbled toward him and he put his arms around her.

"I figure we'll share the blanket." He lifted and freed her hair, lingering to rub the strands between his thumb and forefinger, much as she'd done to Caleb's mane.

She hoped she hadn't made the horse as nervous as Jesse was making her. "Share…as in you have a turn, then I have one? Or do you mean we'd be using it at the same time?"

He looked as if he wanted to laugh. "Which do you prefer?"

"Whichever is more practical," she said, and was startled to see her breath mingle with his in the cold air.

"Of course." His eyes probed hers and then he lowered his gaze to her lips. "I'd better get back to the fire."

He was already doing a fine job of heating the room, or at least her. Warmth filled her chest and pooled in her belly. For a split second she thought he might kiss her again. Was he waiting for a signal from her? God, she was so bad at this.

No, the kiss hadn't meant anything. He'd been relieved to find her. It had just happened. Anyway, it would be a mistake. Getting physical wouldn't end well. It never had for her. Not once. She'd be disappointed, things would get awkward and then they'd be stuck here together for who knew how long.

"Maybe I should tackle—" Her voice sounded weak and shaky. She cleared her throat and moved away before trying again. "I saw a stack of old newspapers. I should crumple some."

"We'll need them eventually," he agreed, and checked the fire. "Your jeans are wet. You should take them off."

She glanced down. They were soaked. How had she not noticed? "I can't do that."

"We'll hang them near the stove," he said in a casual tone, his focus remaining on the growing flames. "They'll dry faster than they will plastered to you."

"I don't have other clothes to change into."

"You have the blanket."

"But we're going to share it."

He turned his head toward her, one dark brow lifted in amusement. "So you've decided."

"Stop that." She sounded as though she were five.

"What?"

"You're teasing me."

"I am," he said with a smile that was far from contrite. "But you'd still be better off losing the jeans."

She did the only thing she could—she ignored him. After busying herself with collecting and crumpling newspaper, she found part of a torn T-shirt that was probably meant as a rag. Unused and relatively soil free, it was perfect for dusting off the two benches and the cot. She picked up the sole pillow, stood at the open door and tried to shake out the dust and bits of dried leaves that had accumulated inside the faded pillowcase. No matter, her head wouldn't be going anywhere near that thing.

Now that she knew her jeans were drenched, they'd become horribly uncomfortable. She had the miserable feeling that as long as they were wet she'd never fully warm up. It made no sense to have a cot but no blankets or sheets. Then again, she doubted anything she'd find here would be acceptable to have pressed against her body.

The mere idea made her shudder. "Why is this shack here?" she asked Jesse, who'd done a great job with the fire during the twenty minutes she'd spent ignoring him.

"It's used for fishing trips, emergencies, a place to spend the night if you're mending fences." A flame licked out of the stove, narrowly missing him. He leaned back and shut the metal door with a loud clang.

"Are we that far from civilization?"

Jesse straightened, stretched out his long lean form and dusted his hands together. "Yep, guess you're at my mercy."

9

SHE STARED AT HIM with her serious gray eyes, then blinked and huffed. "I'm so glad I can amuse you."

Jesse smiled, pleased that she'd started to loosen up. The impulsive kiss he'd laid on her could've done some damage. No way he could explain what had gotten into him. Other than he'd been relieved to see that she was okay. Fortunately, it seemed she was willing to forget it, not read too much into his rashness and move on.

Trouble was, he wouldn't mind kissing her again.

It finally occurred to him that he was staring at her lips, and he got down to the business of removing his other glove. "As the crow flies we aren't too far from Safe Haven or the Heber ranch. This type of line shack is a holdover from the old West."

She huddled closer to the stove. "It looks it. You'd think the place would be better equipped."

"Nowadays you can have them built log-cabin style with most of the luxuries of a resort. If you've got money to burn that is." He tossed his glove at the cot. "Cy used to like to tip the bottle back now and again. His wife wouldn't have it so he'd sneak out here. Kept his whiskey right under that…"

Jesse lifted the frying pan and kettle, then the bucket. Sure enough, there was a fifth of Jim Beam. He picked up the bottle of bourbon and held it to the light. Half-full. God bless Cy.

"You're not going to drink that."

"Well, darlin'…" he drawled, giving her a wink. "I'd wager we'll both be a little happy before the night's over."

She wrinkled her nose. "Not me—" she paused "—darlin'."

At least he'd gotten her to crack a small smile. "Need help pulling off those jeans?"

Her brows shot up and she stared at him as if she didn't know what to say. He figured she probably didn't. She wasn't as uptight as he'd initially thought, but she seemed to be oddly innocent, as if the world she saw was completely different from the world of an ordinary Joe like him. It made him wonder what life had been like for her, growing up with that kind of naïveté. Combined with the level of smarts that were required to be a computer software engineer, it was a peculiar mix. Interesting. Appealing.

He hooked his boot around the leg of a nearby stool and pulled it closer to the fire. "You think I'm joking but that denim is soaked. It's gonna need to be peeled off you."

"What about *your* jeans?"

"They're only wet to the knees, but they're coming off right now."

She pulled the blanket tighter around her shoulders. He'd expected her to turn away. Instead she stared with owlish fascination as he set the bottle on the floor then unbuckled his belt.

Well, hell, he wasn't about to do a striptease. "How are your feet?"

"My feet?"

"They have to be cold. Take off your boots and massage your toes. Get the circulation going." He nudged the stool toward her and got one of the narrow benches for himself.

She dragged the stool farther away from him, tested its stability by pushing on the seat then trying to rock it back and forth. Apparently satisfied she wouldn't fall on her cute little ass, she slowly lowered herself, arranging the blanket so she wasn't sitting on it.

He waited until she bowed her head to unlace her boots before he unzipped his fly.

The sound brought her head up. "You're really going to take those off?"

"Will it offend you?"

She vigorously shook her head, then lowered her lids and went back to removing her boots. Her teeth still chattered sporadically, and it killed him that he couldn't make her warmer.

Although he wouldn't admit it to her, he was pretty damn cold himself. He'd hoped to find a wool blanket—even a moth-eaten one would do. But the place seemed bare. Then, too, he hadn't looked around much since they'd had some light.

Last time he'd been out here was to repair some fence for Cy because the old man had been forced to let his help go. Had to be about five years ago when Jesse had come home on leave. Back then the shack was better stocked and he'd stayed on a couple days after the job was finished just to be alone. His family never knew. They would've been hurt.

With his jeans half-open, he picked up the lantern and moved it around. Peering into the dark corners where a broken camping chair and empty crates had been shoved. The soft glow was better than nothing, but not by much.

"Is something wrong?"

"Just having a look."

"You want the flashlight?"

"Yeah, that might be better." He found a hook near the cot and hung the lantern from it.

She'd taken off a glove and was holding out the flashlight.

Her skin was red, mostly her fingers. They were trembling but that wasn't what had him worried.

"Let's see." He stuck the flashlight under his arm, took her hand and probed her palm and knuckle area. "Can you feel this?"

"Yes."

"No numbness?"

She pulled away. "It actually hurts a little so I know I don't have frostbite."

"I didn't think so but it can happen faster than you think. Now your feet."

One boot was off. Her red striped socks didn't look wet. She wiggled her toes. "Cold but fine. I was sitting on Candy Cane most of the time." Her gaze lowered to his boots. "We should be worried about you."

He retrieved the flashlight and flipped the switch. The beam landed on the metal bucket, which reminded him… "First I need to go outside again," he said, grabbing the bucket.

"Why?"

"Collect some snow."

She frowned briefly, then nodded. "Need help?"

"I got it." He glanced over his shoulder toward the cot. "If you find another bucket or pot that I missed, let me know."

Clearly no one had used the place in a long time and hadn't bothered to leave it ready for an emergency. Sometimes high school kids used the abandoned shacks to party, but they obviously hadn't found this one or the whiskey would be gone.

Like many other small ranchers trapped in the poor economy, the Hebers had ended up selling most of their herd shortly after Jesse had returned to duty. And since Cy had given up booze, the place likely had been forgotten.

After zipping his fly, he prepared himself for the cold outside. He bowed his head to block the icy wind from stinging his face and scooped snow into the bucket. The small shack was chock-full of memories, most of them good, some not. He'd been going through a tough time five years ago, confused about his future and the lack of direction in his life. Staying out here alone had been peaceful, but he'd returned to the Sundance without answers.

Before going inside he stopped to check on the mare. The door opened and Shea poked her head out.

"Is Candy Cane all right?" she asked.

"She's fine." He stroked the bay's neck. "I see you found a pot."

Shea glanced down. "Oh, yes, here." He took it before she walked out into the snow in her stocking feet. "Are you sure she's okay?"

"Yes. You're letting heat escape." He forced her to back up by setting the bucket down just inside, and noted the glint of suspicion in her eye as he pulled the door closed.

He hadn't lied. She was a city girl. To her animals were pampered pets. The mare was just fine for now, whereas he and Shea couldn't afford to lose heat. The old stove was efficient but unable to sustain a comfortable temperature without enough logs. They were hurting in that department. He'd have to feed the fire slowly, keep it just warm enough that they didn't freeze. No telling when the weather would let up.

After filling the pot, he stomped the snow off his boots and went back inside. She'd moved closer to the stove. Her other glove and socks were off but she still had her jeans on. Jesse sighed. She was never going to get warm.

"I don't know what you want me to do with the bucket," she said, watching him place the pot on the fire as she rubbed her toes.

"Your job is to keep the blood flowing." He ignored her eye-roll and moved the bucket to the other side of the stove. He left his jacket there to dry, then sat down to unlace his sturdy air-force-issue boots. Normally he wore cowboy boots but not when he flew, especially in winter.

Good thing. His socks were still dry. He left them on, then stood to unzip his fly. Again, her head came up. He wasn't shy or even modest, but Jesus.

"You really wanna watch?" he asked, and then could only chuckle when it looked as if she were debating the matter.

"Are you wearing thermal underwear?" she asked with a casual curiosity that surprised him.

"Yep, but those are coming off, too. Turn your head if you want."

She studied him for a long, drawn-out moment, then bowed her head and massaged her other foot.

He stripped off his jeans, dragged the cot closer to the stove and hung the Levi's off the end. Then he peeled down his cotton thermals and hung them, too, leaving room for her things. It felt good to be free of the wet clinging material. Luckily for everyone, his brown boxers were bone-dry.

Shea sighed loudly.

He looked up and found her gaze focused on his fly. Not his cock precisely, but the same vicinity.

"What?" he asked slowly, heat stirring low in his belly. Another few seconds and she'd figure out exactly what was on his mind.

"You're just being sensible."

Did she sound disappointed, or was it wishful thinking on his part? "As opposed to…" He drew out the words, then waited, not happy that his body continued to tense. The last thing he wanted to do was scare her. He casually walked around the other side of the cot to get to his seat.

"I'm being stupid." She rose and let the blanket slide down her back and onto the stool.

Lifting the hem of her jacket so she could see what she was doing, she unsnapped her jeans and drew down the zipper, without hesitation, as if it were perfectly normal for her to undress in front of him. She wiggled as she forced the wet denim past her hips. Leaving on the beige thermals she wore underneath, she then sat to finish pulling off the jeans.

And he'd been worried about the kiss, or that he'd scared her? She hadn't even tried to hide behind the stove or asked him to turn around. In fact, she was treating him like he was onc of her girlfriends.

Irritated, he sat down again and watched, waiting for her to chuck the thermals.

This time her fingers hesitated at the waistband. She fixed him with a stare as frigid as the outside temperature. "You really wanna watch?" she asked, throwing his words back at him.

"You really want an answer?" He let out a laugh, gladly suffering her steely gaze. "All right." He swung around and gave her his back.

"When do you think we'll be able to leave?"

"Hard to say. If the snow doesn't let up overnight, I'll go to the plane at first light and use the radio."

"On foot?" She'd moved away, judging by the muffled tone of her voice. Probably hanging up her jeans.

"Depends how deep the snow is."

She stayed silent long enough that he was about to turn around when she said, "How will radioing help us? Or is it simply a matter of reporting in?"

"The wind seems to be dying down some. I'll let Cole know how it looks out here and he'll come get us."

"How?"

"Snowmobiles, if necessary." He sensed her tension and wanted to see what she was up to. The stool's legs scraped the wood floor. "The truth is he'll show up no matter what, so no need to worry. Can I turn around now?"

"Yes," she said so softly, the crackle of the fire nearly drowned her out.

He didn't need to see the slump of her shoulders to know her mood had shifted. She'd rewrapped the blanket around her body and stared idly at the stove. "We're not in trouble," he said. "If I thought we were, that would've trumped the risk of someone coming after us. I knew we'd find shelter."

She stretched her bare legs out in front of her, toward the stove. Her thighs were covered by the blanket, but not her pale shapely calves and slim ankles. He tried not to stare. He'd hate for her to think that his judgment call had been motivated by a personal agenda. The storm had hit quickly, its ferocity unexpected, and for sure his brothers had their hands full back at the Sundance. To have unnecessarily brought them out in this mess would have been irresponsible.

"I feel so horribly guilty," she said after a while. "I should've listened to Annie. She didn't want me to go after Caleb. She was distracted and I took advantage of the situation."

He'd wondered what had happened. Didn't make sense that Annie would let Shea run off like she had. "Look, we're okay. Everyone's been notified. They know you're with me, so they won't worry."

"No, they just all think I'm a total idiot. Probably won't trust me with the animals anymore."

"I suspect they think you're a very kind and compassionate woman who was concerned about a horse."

She glanced at him, then seemed to concentrate on her toes, curling them toward the stove. "What about you?"

"I definitely don't think you're an idiot."

Her lips lifted in a faint smile. "I was referring to you being collateral damage. You're stuck here because of me."

Jesse sucked in a breath. That was true because he never would've landed on that field if he hadn't seen her. But he sure wasn't going to admit it. "There's another way to look at the situation. Maybe I was meant to fly over at that particular moment and spot you."

"So we'd end up here…stranded…together."

He shrugged a shoulder. Sounded weird put that way.

"You're talking about fate."

"Whatever."

"I don't believe in that."

He didn't, either. "You hungry?"

"No." She drew her legs up until they disappeared under the blanket. Hugging her knees, she continued to stare at the stove as if she could see the fire. "I can't even think about food."

"You'll have to eat sometime."

"What?" She made a face. "That canned stuff in the corner?"

"I doubt it'll come to that. I have jerky, trail mix and dried fruit in my bag."

That seemed to spark her attention. She looked over at him. "Do you think Candy Cane would eat the dried fruit?"

He snorted. "If I know Annie, that mare was well fed this morning. I suspect she had a full belly when you left. Mine not so much."

"I meant I'd give her my share."

"Do you know how much a horse eats?" he asked, and she blushed. "We'll have to conserve our food. Water we'll have plenty of."

"And whiskey," she murmured.

He'd almost forgotten. "You want a drink?"

She shook her head. "I don't know why I brought it up."

"I'm having a shot." He stood and was reminded he wore only boxers when she darted a glance at him, then quickly looked away.

"I don't suppose there's any coffee fit to drink." She

twisted around to study the shelved cans, giving him another tempting view of bare legs.

"I'll look." First, he checked on the progress of his thermals. They normally dried quickly but he was asking for too much. Still damp. "There should be a pair of tin cups around here somewhere."

The wind had died down, at least it had stopped rattling the shack's old frame, and just maybe the place would still be standing by the time they got out of here. Nah, he really wasn't worried about the place. Though carpentry had never been his or Cole's strong suit. And certainly not when they'd been eighteen and nineteen.

But when he'd spent those two days by himself he'd reinforced the door frame, repaired a few loose boards and patched three places on the roof. He'd already figured by then the shack wouldn't be used much, but he'd been driven to use his hands. His overtaxed brain had needed the distraction.

He should've been on top of the world at the time. Everyone else thought so. And they were right. Twenty-six years old, a pilot in the United States Air Force, months away from being made captain. Most guys who'd been through all the training and jumped all the hurdles to sit in an air force cockpit were lifers. Flying in the military wasn't something you did on a whim. It was a passion, a calling. Even though he hadn't been among the hotshots and flyboys, he'd been necessary in the scheme of things. He did a job that mattered and that had felt damn good. But most of the other pilots also called the military their home. They didn't have the Sundance waiting for them on the other side of the world. If only that feeling of being needed, being an integral part of something bigger, was as true at the ranch as it had been in the air.... But that wasn't how it had worked out.

"Look at me sitting here," Shea said. "I should be helping."

He jerked, realizing that he'd been staring at the row of

canned goods. "Nah." He shook off the haze and gestured for her to stay seated. "I don't need help." He raked a hand through his short hair. "There might be some coffee in this canister," he said, a flicker of memory bringing him to a crouch as he picked up the aluminum container. "It'll probably be stale but we might be desperate enough."

She'd already gotten to her feet. "I'm assuming you know how to brew over an open fire. I can at least add more logs."

"I'll take care of it."

"You get the coffee ready."

"Shea, wait."

Juggling three logs that she'd already gathered, she slowly straightened.

He was hoping to avoid this conversation. "One log at a time, okay?"

Her gaze went first to the pair of logs he removed from the cradle of her arms, and then to the small reserve pile. "Oh, we don't have enough wood."

"We need to go easy on how much we use, that's all."

"I should've realized..." She shook her head. "Let's forget the coffee," she said, returning the log to the stack.

Jesse blew out a stream of air. He could still see his breath but the shack was warmer. "We have to be sensible, but that doesn't rule out coffee."

"I vote for the whiskey," she said, struggling with the sagging blanket.

"Hopefully we'll have both."

He went to work, feeding one of the logs to the fire then assessing the coffee situation. There was about a cup's worth of grounds. No doubt old, but he was willing to give it a shot. Not all the snow he'd collected had melted yet, but there was enough to get a pot brewing.

Shea had found the tin cups and was dubiously inspecting the insides when he turned around.

"Just blow out the dust," he said, picking up the bottle of Jim Beam. "Think of all the crap we ate off the floor as babies."

"True." She peeked into the bucket. "But since we're in no short supply of snow, I think I'll go a step further."

He watched with amusement as she daintily used her fingers to scoop snow into each cup, then swished it around. Once she'd scrubbed the cups to her satisfaction, she scanned the room, her gaze hesitating on some rags they'd found, before she set down the still-damp cups.

He unscrewed the cap on the whiskey and reached for one.

"I'm not done with them." She'd left the blanket in a heap on the stool and was unzipping her jacket.

There he went again, staring at her legs. Man, he had to get a grip on himself. He'd been lucky she'd let the kiss slide.

When she picked up a cup and lifted the hem of her shirt, exposing skimpy bikini panties, Jesse tipped the entire bottle to his lips.

10

DESPITE THE MISTAKES she'd made since this morning, Shea had been able to compartmentalize so that everything had seemed manageable. Until this moment.

Because Jesse was standing right there in his boxers…and he had a hard-on….

She didn't dare look again.

Taking a deep, even breath, she focused on wiping out the cups, making sure she didn't leave any lint behind. Now her hem was damp. So what, it would dry soon enough. She pulled the black flannel shirt down and smoothed it over her belly, the whole time keeping her eyes downcast.

She'd lived with a man for nearly two years, after all, so she was familiar with erections, for goodness' sake. Admittedly, though, Jesse's was quite impressive.

Good grief, she could *not* look there again.

Keeping her gaze averted, she slowly lifted her chin. Then chanced a peek.

Jesse used the back of his sleeve to wipe his mouth. She was relieved when his eyes didn't meet hers…except…where was *he* looking? God.

In spite of her best intention, her gaze dropped to his fly.

She tried to swallow but couldn't summon enough saliva. Oh, this was a problem. A very big problem.

"Shea?"

"I decided against the coffee," she said, instinctively squeezing her thighs together. "I think I'll try to get some sleep instead." Oh, she so wanted to snatch up that blanket and wrap it around herself, but it wasn't fair to him. It was his turn.

"Here, have some of this." He poured the whiskey into the cup and passed it to her. "I know you're not much of a drinker, take your time, sip on it for a while and—"

She downed the entire contents. Before she could finish swallowing, she started to cough. Not a small polite cough, but a horrible, out-of-control wheezing shudder that shook her whole body.

Embarrassed, she covered her face with her hands.

"Hey." Jesse pried her fingers away and pushed the cold tin cup against her palm. "Try this."

"No, I'm never ever going to—" She coughed again.

"It's water. Melted snow. It won't kill you."

"How do you know?" she murmured, completely miserable.

He smiled. "Guess you'll have to trust me."

She managed to get the liquid down, which did help lessen the burning in her throat. "I did, and look how well that turned out."

"In my defense, you weren't supposed to gulp it."

"It's still your fault," she was able to utter without coughing.

"How?"

"By standing there—" she took another cautious sip, eyes downcast, and waved a hand in his general direction "—like that."

"Ah." He noisily cleared his throat. "Perfectly normal

healthy male reaction. It's not like I planned it." He turned to head toward the cot. "I'll put my Levi's back on."

"Are they dry?"

He hesitated. "No."

"Well, then that's silly." Moving closer to the stove, she put her hands out to warm them, and longingly eyed the blanket. It had made a huge difference. "Use that instead. It's your turn, anyway."

"I'm sorry, Shea. I am. We'll be here awhile and I don't want it to be awkward."

Had he already forgotten about the kiss? "No problem." She couldn't look at him but concentrated on rubbing her hands together. "Really, I understand. I know it's not personal—" She gasped when she felt something touch her shoulders.

It was Jesse, trying to drape the blanket around her.

"No," she said, attempting to evade him, except she was trapped between him and the stove. "I'm not cold, really, just my hands."

"You're shivering." He ran his palms down her arms, then stepped back.

Clutching the blanket to her breasts, she turned to face him. "This solves only one problem," she said, hoping she didn't have to elaborate. "We'd both benefit from you covering up."

"Ah." His lips twitched. "Problem is, that goes both ways."

This wasn't good, him standing so close…her facing him. She could feel the heat spreading from her pelvis in all directions, not embarrassment exactly, but a sexual response that wasn't listening at all to the voice in her head that insisted she settle down. How could she process what he was saying when she couldn't think straight?

She glanced down at her weak knees—at least they only

felt wobbly. When she lifted her gaze she saw that he was a bit too interested in her legs.

"Oh." His words were starting to make sense. She blinked, and instinctively glanced at his fly. "You said it wasn't personal."

"No, you said that." He rubbed the back of his head, his cheeks puffing out as he exhaled. "Do us both a favor," he said gruffly. "Keep the blanket."

"Jesse…" She started to touch his arm, then reconsidered.

"What?" He wouldn't look at her.

"Thank you…for everything."

"Sure. No problem." He went around the stove to the cot and picked up his jeans.

"Wait."

"I'm going outside to get more snow."

"Please, don't."

"We have to maintain a water supply."

She didn't want him to be angry with her. Or for him to misunderstand her reaction to him. If she let him leave he'd probably stay outside for as long as he could, all because of her and her awkward response. She'd never known what to say or do at the right time. "That's not what I meant."

He shook out the jeans, and sat on the cot. Holding up the trousers, he leaned back and started to cram a leg in when she heard a rip. Jesse froze. Their eyes met for a split second, and then another loud tear. He jerked upright but not before the cot gave.

"Goddammit." He threw up an arm as he fell backward, and Shea caught his hand. He had a good eighty or ninety pounds on her and almost pulled her down with him. She held on tight, leaning back to use her own weight as leverage until he was able to stand.

The look on his face was priceless. Pressing her lips together, she backed away and tried not to laugh.

"You think that was funny?" He didn't seem amused. "I was going to be a gentleman and give you the cot tonight."

"Thank you for testing it for me." She managed to keep a straight face but when he caught her wrist and pulled her toward him, she let out a yelp.

Momentarily panicked, she started to fight him. His expression stopped her. This was Jesse…but it wasn't. The heat that had just started to calm flared again, licked up her spine and filled her chest. She couldn't seem to speak. Her dry mouth felt as if it was filled with cotton. She couldn't look away, either.

His hooded brown eyes seemed darker, more intense, and his nostrils flared slightly. "I want to kiss you," he said quietly. "I'm going to kiss you," he amended. "You have to tell me no."

His arm came around her waist, and she melted against him. If she'd wanted to move it would've been impossible.

Oddly, she wanted to stay right where she was, letting him trace her lips with his forefinger. The awareness coursing through her was both terrifying and exciting, nothing she'd ever experienced before. Even though sex with Brian had never been good, intellectually she thought she knew how she was supposed to feel. This wasn't like anything she'd imagined.

She swallowed around the lump in her throat. How long had it been since she'd been kissed? A year, two years? Long before Brian had moved out, their physical relationship had died. They might as well have been brother and sister or platonic roommates. The way she felt with her breasts pressed against Jesse's chest was anything but sisterly.

He dipped his head and brushed his lips across hers. "Last chance."

She took a shuddering breath, not understanding her sudden frustration. Outrage or reticence or even fear would be far more appropriate responses. But frustration?

His other arm came around her so that both his hands rested on the curve of her backside. She fisted the blanket so tightly that her nails dug into her palms. Her whole body shifted, yet he hadn't moved her…so what…?

To her utter astonishment, she'd pushed up onto the tips of her toes. He touched his tongue to the corner of her mouth, and her lips seemed to part without her permission. Still he didn't rush, just tasted and teased, chasing away her confusion until she softened her mouth and opened wide enough to invite him inside.

Groaning, he pulled her closer to his lean, hard body. The thickness and heat of his erection was startling, but she didn't want him to stop. She just stood there and let him kiss her, slowly, thoroughly, as she'd never been kissed before. The dark stubble on his chin and jaw lightly grazed her skin, and how could she possibly find that arousing? Nothing made sense.

When he drew his head back, her vision was so bleary she could barely see his face.

"I'm pretty sure you don't mind me kissing you," he said, then gently brushed his lips across hers. "But you're not kissing me back."

"You're going to be disappointed," she whispered, her voice shaky.

He stilled and gave her a long puzzled look. "Disappointed?"

Blinking away the remnants of her hazy vision, she nodded and looked him directly in the eyes, hoping he'd understand.

"You won't disappoint me." His expression softened. "I can promise you that."

"I wasn't referring only to myself." Her gaze didn't waver. "I'll be disappointed, too."

His brows shot up, his hands at her back slackened and he choked out a laugh.

"The kissing was nice," she admitted, mildly startled that she wished he was still kissing her. "But going further will just mess everything up. We both know sex never lives up to expectations."

"Uh..." He studied her face. "No, somehow that one got by me."

Shea sighed. Yes, she was often clueless. She knew that, but the male ego was one thing she did understand. Good grief, she hoped he didn't mistake her edict for a challenge. She'd stated a simple fact, that's all.

Her gaze snagged on his damp mouth. He truly had great lips, perfectly shaped and just the right amount of fullness. Darn it. Maybe she should've let him kiss her a bit longer before she brought up the harsh truth.

"Well, I'm glad we cleared that up," she said, moving back until he released her.

"Yeah, clear as mud." He gave her a crooked smile. "I don't know who you've—" Stopping himself, he passed a hand over his face then exhaled slowly. "Think I'll go get that snow."

He grabbed the bucket and was out the door before she could remind him he'd forgotten to put on his jeans.

THE SKY WAS STILL dark gray, but not black like it had been earlier. Jesse squinted up at the falling snow and then to the pine trees flanking the shack, their branches hanging heavy with ice. He hated sleet. Give him the good ol' powdery variety any day.

And a woman he could understand.

Not that he could figure out most of them. With Shea, though, he was way out of his depth. No matter. If he didn't go back inside, his pecker was liable to freeze off.

Shit. How could a man forget to put on his Levi's?

Before he started shivering like a damn fool, he carried the bucket of snow inside. He was immediately greeted by Shea holding open the blanket. "Keep that on," he said, walking past her to place the bucket close to the heat.

"Don't be stubborn."

"I'm being sensible." He picked up his jeans. "You not getting your way doesn't make me stubborn."

She yanked the Levi's out of his hands. "They aren't dry. Not even close. How rational does that make you?"

Surprised, he noticed the slight lift of her chin. "Good. Something lit a fire under your butt. We could use all the heat we can get." He'd had a better way of warming up but that obviously wasn't going to work. "Give me back my jeans."

"No." She tossed them on the cot, then blocked his avenue to retrieve them and held up the blanket again.

He thought for a moment. "Okay, have it your way." He turned around, smiling when she couldn't see his face, waiting for her to drape the blanket on his shoulders.

She did, her hands tentative and hovering. "Have you got it?"

Before she could move away, he caught the edge of the material and shifted positions to face her. "So, how do you see this playing out?"

"This?" Moistening her lips, she took a step back.

"One blanket, limited supply of wood. The wind has subsided, the snow has let up some, but not enough…" He kept his gaze level with hers, resisting the urge to look down at her bare legs. "Most likely we'll be here all night."

"Yes, but this isn't new information. We've already considered the possibility."

"True, but we haven't discussed how to *rationally* make our night as comfortable as possible."

"We have to behave like adults."

"I figured that was a given." He smiled when her gaze

sharpened into a slight glare. He couldn't help it then, and glanced down at her legs, to that sweet spot, that narrow strip of space where her thighs didn't touch. It was a turn-on for him, had been since he'd been old enough to appreciate the opposite sex.

Shea took a deep shuddering breath that snapped him back to the conversation. "That wasn't a challenge," she said softly, "what I told you earlier."

"What?" He had no business playing dumb. Gawking at her like he had, he deserved to be called out. "I didn't interpret it as a challenge." He wished she'd take the damn blanket. Not just to cover up, but he wanted her warm. "Naturally it crossed my mind that you haven't been with the right guys—"

She rolled her eyes.

"Hey, like I said, it was a natural reaction. Sex is great. Usually. Sometimes not so much. I'm speaking in general terms...."

With a resigned expression, she shook her head. "We're conditioned to assume that it's this spectacular event that we should— What's that look for? You think I'm a virgin."

"Nope. I'm not thinking anything." He tapped a forefinger at his temple. "Totally empty in here."

"I've had sex before. I even lived with someone for almost two years."

He frowned, taking a second to mull over a disturbing thought. "A guy?"

"Yes," she said through gritted teeth. "A guy. Maybe that was the problem. I joined the wrong team."

"I reckon that's a possibility." Jesse grinned when she rolled her eyes, but he didn't miss the goose bumps on her legs. The shack was still chilly. "Hey, I'll talk this thing to death if you want, but only if you take the blanket."

"I don't want to discuss it anymore. My sex life, or lack

thereof, is no one's business. I just wanted to clarify the situation."

"Right." He swung the blanket off his shoulders and onto hers before she could object. "Here's the thing," he said, carefully tucking the material under her chin. "You might not think about sex or be easily turned on, but I'm not immune like you. Having to look at your bare legs is sheer torture."

Her eyes narrowed. "Really?"

He could've pointed out that she'd already seen the proof but thought better of it. "You're very attractive, and I'm cold, not dead." He watched her expression slide into skepticism. "Is that so hard to believe?"

"Frankly, yes."

Man, he'd love a minute alone with the guy responsible for her self-doubt. "Look, you owe me one for landing the Cessna and bringing you here. Can we agree on that?"

"We can," she said cautiously.

"I'm calling in the favor. You keep that blanket around you until it's time to bed down."

"Then?"

"We share it."

She studied him as though she guessed he was up to something. "The two-people, one-blanket version?"

"Shouldn't be a problem, right? You're not interested in sex." He shrugged and turned to check if the fire was ready for more wood. "Or me."

"I don't believe I put it quite that way."

"But that's the bottom line." He chose one of the larger logs. Once they were both under the blanket he could afford to let the temperature drop some. "Right?"

"I suppose." She moved to look inside the stove, keeping her gaze on the fire and away from him. "No, that's not accurate." She took a deep shuddering breath. "If I *were* interested, someone like you would appeal to me."

"Ah, I feel better already."

"Come on. I'm just trying to be truthful."

He slid her a sideways glance and smiled. "So what happened with the guy you were living with?"

"Brian? He moved out," she said in a matter-of-fact tone. "I don't blame him in the least. He had the good sense to do what I was too lethargic to do myself."

"How enlightened."

A faint smile tugged at her lips. "My realization hardly happened overnight."

He wondered how long it had been since thc breakup. Could be why she was here instead of spending the holidays at home. "How did you meet? In college?"

She shook her head. "At work."

"You both still at the same company?"

"Yes, but our paths don't cross much. Anyway, he has a new girlfriend who works in accounting." Shea seemed genuinely indifferent, and then she squinted at something behind him. "What's that in the corner behind the crate?"

He thought she might be trying to change the subject until she clutched his arm when he turned to look.

"Be careful. It might be an animal. It wasn't there before," she said, her fingers digging into his biceps.

If it was an animal, they'd have known it before now. He grabbed the flashlight and shined the beam at the dark lump. That's right, he remembered the crack in the wall and how he'd blocked it with a bedroll. Could be useful, but he had no idea what kind of shape it was in by now.

He hesitated telling her what it was. She'd move away as soon as he did. "It's a sleeping bag."

"How do you know?"

"I put it there last time I was here."

"Oh." She stayed where she was, her hand still wrapped around his arm. "I could've sworn it wasn't there before."

He turned his head to look at her face. "It's in shadow, easy to miss."

Her tongue slipped out, and she ran it across her upper lip. "I'm not volunteering to inspect it."

"Chicken," he murmured.

"I am," she whispered back, although he had the feeling she wasn't talking about the sleeping bag anymore. Not with that look in her eyes, and the way she was staring at his mouth as she swayed toward him. "But I don't want to be."

He caught her shoulders, pretty sure he knew what she wanted. Dammit, he'd sworn he wouldn't do this. If he'd misread her, he'd regret it for a very long time. "Shea…"

"Please."

The yearning in her eyes stirred something primal inside him. He lowered his head and kissed her.

11

WHAT WAS WRONG with her? Shea knew better. She'd been lucky the first time. Their earlier kiss had been about the moment. Something easy to explain and dismiss. But now? The night would inevitably end in yet more disillusionment, then the rest of her stay would be awkward. Every time she saw Jesse again she'd regret this momentary weakness. She'd die a little whenever he averted his gaze, unable to look at her without remembering the most frustrating night of his life.

So she simply stood there, trying so hard to just let this part be perfect, a memory to take with her before things changed. Angry that her body wanted so much more. Her chest tightened and she struggled against the urge to squeeze her thighs together. She was getting damp there, more than damp.

"We shouldn't do this," she whispered against his mouth.

He took his time, nibbling lightly at her lips, barely touching her yet exciting her as no one had ever done before. "Isn't this what you wanted?"

"Yes. No." She struggled for air. "I don't know," she said brokenly, alarmed at the burning ache in the pit of her stomach.

His arms came around her, pulling her against his body, one hand stroking her back, the other tangling in her hair.

She let out a gasp at the feel of his thick erection pressed against her belly.

She didn't know how or when it happened…only a second ago she'd been clutching the blanket at her throat. But her hands had moved to his chest and were alternately kneading and clawing at his flannel shirt.

His tongue parted her lips, and she accepted him inside, confusion and fear fading along with her hesitancy. He wasn't rough or rushed but seemed more interested in paying attention to detail. After a thorough exploration of her mouth, he returned to biting softly at her lips, then her chin and jaw, and finally trailing his damp mouth down her throat to the collar of her shirt.

Only her top button had been left undone and she held her breath, waiting to see what he'd do next. He lifted his head and smiled at her. Adrenaline shot through her body, and she had the crazy impulse to drag his mouth down to her breasts, urge him to give her tight achy nipples the release they needed.

"Go ahead," he whispered. "Do it."

She stared at him in shock. Had she spoken her thoughts out loud? No, she couldn't have….

He glanced down at her hands, one of them still clawing at the flannel, the other fisting his shirt. "I'd rather you unfasten the buttons."

"Oh." She snatched back her hands.

He caught her wrist. "It's okay."

"Did I tear it?" Judging by the sting in her cheeks, her face must be flaming red. "Oh, God, I'm sorry—"

Touching a finger to her lips, he silenced her. Then he slid his hand down her neck to the valley between her breasts where her jacket gaped open. His probing thumb grazed her nipple. Her whole body had started quivering. It was no use pretending he hadn't noticed. She could blame it on the chilly air. Except she didn't feel cold anymore, her internal temperature had risen to a fever pitch, and she supposed he knew that, too.

"Jesse, wait," she said, when he started to steer her captured hand to his chest. "This will end in disappointment and there'll be no taking anything back."

"Have I disappointed you so far?"

"No," she said.

"Have I done anything you don't like?"

"No, but—"

"Does this feel like disappointment to you?" He guided her hand lower until her palm pressed his arousal.

She swallowed. He pulsed against her, and she jumped, jerking away her hand. Her breath came in short, hard gasps. She helplessly stared down at the bulge behind the thin cotton fly, wishing she hadn't been so hasty. She wanted to touch him more but she couldn't make herself do it.

"That doesn't prove anything," she murmured, lifting her gaze to his face.

The pity she saw in his eyes caught her off guard. She staggered back a step. Humiliation flooded her chest and belly. She was no match for someone like Jesse. She felt sick suddenly. Worse, she felt as if she were fifteen again, thrown out into a fast and confusing world she didn't yet understand.

"Shea, what's the matter?"

She shoved him away and searched blindly for the stool. For a second she thought about running for the door but he'd follow her outside for sure. Anyway, what good would it do to run into the snow besides prove she was that same inexperienced young girl who felt desperately out of sync with normal life? The only thing that would get her would be more pity.

"Dammit, I'm not going to hurt you." He caught her flailing arm. "Tell me what's wrong."

"I need something to drink." She twisted her arm until he was forced to release her. "Where's the whiskey?"

"Shea. Jesus, I'm sorry. I misread the situation." He exhaled sharply. "I swear to you I would've stopped if that's what you wanted."

"The whiskey?"

His expression bleak, he gave her a long searching look and then walked past her.

She wrapped the blanket tightly around her body and sat huddled on the stool close to the stove and waited, not daring to see what he was doing behind her. She'd done it again. Muddled things when she hadn't meant to. It was as if she spoke a different language, and there were no translators. Jesse was being nice, and she had to confess that the proof of his attraction was very compelling. Why wouldn't her stupid brain let her have this? It wasn't fair.

"Here." Apparently he didn't trust her with the bottle. He passed her a tin cup barely a quarter full.

She took a tiny sip and found he'd already watered it down. Although he had no business making that decision for her, she couldn't summon the energy to object. Taking another sip, she watched him pick up his jeans and pull them on. They couldn't be dry yet but she didn't say a word.

He lifted the sleeping bag out from behind the wooden crate, using the flashlight to inspect it. She saw now how they'd missed it earlier. Most of it had disappeared into a gap where two boards should've met at the corner. They probably had once but the lumber was warped now and already she could feel a slight draft the sleeping bag had efficiently blocked.

She set down the cup. "Would you say the cot is beyond repair?"

Jesse swung the beam of the flashlight on the torn canvas. "Yep."

"How about if I tear off pieces to plug that gap in the wall?"

"You'll probably need the knife." He motioned with his chin in the direction of the pot and frying pan. "Take the flashlight."

She got up, leaving the blanket on the stool so it wouldn't get in her way. He held out the flashlight without looking at her. God, she hoped he wasn't angry. None of what happened had been his fault. Which was exactly why he had every right to be upset. Trouble was, she didn't know how to fix it.

"That's okay. You keep the light. I'd rather avoid any surprises in the sleeping bag," she said. "Who knows what kind of crawly thing could have gotten in there." He still wouldn't look at her. "Assuming you still plan on sharing it with me."

He glanced over now. "If it looks okay, it's all yours." His gaze dropped to her legs, then quickly flicked to the blanket. "Your jeans and thermals might be dry," he murmured, turning back to the sleeping bag.

She should've already checked but she'd forgotten. She scooped up her cup and took the last sip of the watered whiskey. Then she moved to the cot, felt her jeans, which were still very damp, then used the dim glow of the lantern to rip the canvas into large serviceable pieces. She'd forgotten the knife, but it turned out she didn't need it.

"The sleeping bag is fine," Jesse said from directly behind her. "Give me some of that and I'll plug the wall."

She straightened, pressing a hand to her lower back, which was strained from stooping too long in an unnatural position. "Will this be enough?" she asked, holding out the worn swatches. "Some of them are a bit threadbare."

"They'll work." He took the pieces from her, careful not to so much as brush her fingers with his.

The situation saddened her. She didn't want him walking on eggshells around her. And to her complete astonishment, she missed his casual touching.

They needed to talk. Or at least she needed to do some talking. It wouldn't be easy. At this point she wasn't even sure he'd be willing to listen, or that she was capable of making herself understood. Normally she'd ignore the whole awkward mess and retreat into herself. But she owed Jesse more than that.

She rounded the stove so that she could watch him work while she sucked up her courage. Without thinking, she automatically started to count the floor planks where the light shined, like always, in groups of three. At nine, she caught herself and stopped. If she didn't speak up now, she'd likely crawl into her shell of silence and not reemerge until they left the shack.

"Jesse?" Her voice shook. God, her whole body had started trembling. Maybe she wasn't ready to put herself out there. Or maybe she should've drunk a little more whiskey.

"Yeah?" He crammed in the last piece of canvas.

"Can we talk?"

He hesitated, staying in his crouched position even though he was clearly finished. "I need to go get more snow," he said finally, and rose, dusting his palms together and then wiping them on his jeans. He still hadn't looked at her.

"Okay. Sure." Shc swallowed. "It's nothing."

She watched him pull on his boots, grab his jacket and the bucket, then disappear out the door.

JESSE HAD NEVER been such a yellow-bellied chickenshit in his entire life. Maybe one other time in the eighth grade when Sophie Scroggins had asked him to marry her. He'd left school in the middle of the day and only returned before afternoon homeroom because his mother had threatened to drag him back by his ear.

Interesting that both times he'd wimped out had to do with a female. He glanced back toward the shack. This one in particular really had him tied up in knots. Mostly his doing. He'd been an ass, pushing her too far, and now she wanted to have the dreaded "talk."

Damn.

What made it worse was that he wasn't sure what she wanted to say. That he was a despicable human being? He didn't think so. She'd seemed kind of nervous. Maybe she realized she'd given him mixed signals. The more he thought about it, the more he was convinced that he hadn't totally misread her. She'd been turned on, all right. Probably not as much as him, but she hadn't been indifferent toward him, either. Even though he'd only known Shea a few days, he'd learned a couple of things about reading her. He'd paid attention. The expression of pure joy she'd worn when she'd seen the Christmas tree. The shock that had turned to pleasure then quickly taken a dive to doubt when he'd touched the small of her back. He'd never come across anyone like her before, so maybe this time he'd gotten his signals crossed.

He doubted she lacked experience, though a couple times he'd wondered. She had to be in her mid-twenties and had lived with someone, so she knew what was what. Was it just bad sex that had made her skittish? Hell, he wasn't going to know what was going on in her head until he went back inside and took it like a man.

Jesse shuddered as he made it to the top of the low ridge. It wasn't just the cold wind giving him a chill.

If he screwed things up with her and she hightailed it from the Sundance once they returned, it would put a crimp in Christmas for Annie, upset Rachel, disappoint his mother. And it would downright suck for him, as well.

He squinted in the direction of the Cessna. The plane wasn't visible from where he stood and he hadn't expected it to be, but he saw enough to know it wasn't worth trudging back through the mounting snow to use the radio. Cole would know they were okay. He wouldn't organize a rescue after getting Jesse's message. Not tonight. Tomorrow morning maybe, if the snow hadn't let up.

Darkness was falling quickly, so he turned back toward the shack. If he was careful they could have a fire well into morning. Even if it meant burning the frame of the cot, he'd have to keep the room bearable. Sharing body heat sure wasn't going to be an option.

SHEA WAS SITTING on the stool by the stove. She'd taken off her jacket and draped it across her legs. Her head came up as he crossed the threshold, an expression of surprise and then relief on her face. It made him feel like an even bigger jerk. He should've warned her that he'd be a while.

"Is everything all right?" she asked, giving him a tentative smile.

"I considered trying to get to the Cessna to use the radio again but it's not worth it. Not with the way the snow is still blowing." He carried the bucket to the stove and noticed that she'd laid out the sleeping bag. The blanket was spread overtop.

Stupid place for it. She should've had it wrapped around her shoulders.

"It's kind of weird not having any windows," she said. "From my office at work I have this great view of the San Jose skyline, which I rarely notice. I bet I'll appreciate it more in the future."

He pulled one small bench closer to the stove and farther away from her, and sat down to unlace his boots. His jeans were damp again but they were staying on. "I was rude. I shouldn't have walked out when you wanted to talk. I apologize."

"Apology not accepted," she said, surprising him, and then

shoved the bangs out of her eyes. "I'm the one who needs to apologize. Not you."

Damn, he'd meant to grab the whiskey. He toed off his boots, then got up and found the bottle. If it were up to him, he'd skip the cup but she'd probably want more. He hoped not. Polishing off the Jim Beam by himself would keep him warm. A little numbness would be good, too.

"Do what you want with my apology. It still stands." He poured two shots into a cup and chugged it.

"I need some of that," she said, jumping up and letting her jacket fall to the floor.

He ordered himself not to watch her walk toward the meager kitchen supplies but he didn't have a shred of willpower. Didn't help that her shirt had hitched up and he could see her pink panties riding halfway up her left cheek.

He poured himself another shot.

"You put some water in that?" he asked when she held out her cup to him.

"I don't want it watered down."

"You end up with a headache and no aspirin, it won't be pretty."

"If I get a headache I'll deserve it."

"Suit yourself." He poured her half a shot. "How about some trail mix or jerky?"

She shook her head and bent over to pick up the jacket from the floor.

Jesus. He had to look away.

Reclaiming the stool, she sat down and took a big sip. "Jesse," she said in a sudden rush, "I overreacted earlier and now things are icky between us and I don't have the faintest idea how to fix it."

They stared silently at each other for a moment. He didn't know what to say. "Icky?"

She shrugged a shoulder. "You know what I mean."

"Yeah, I know." He scrubbed at his face, then plowed his hand through his hair. "I don't see what needs fixing," he said, and watched her lower her gaze to her cup, the furrow of her brow deepening. "I promise to be a gentleman, if that's what you're worried about."

"No." She gave him a fleeting look before averting her eyes again. "It's the pity I can't take. I'm fully aware that I'm bad at social interaction, not just with men, but in general and I—"

"Pity? Where's that coming from?"

"Please don't deny it." She sighed. "I don't think you've lied to me yet."

"Damn right I'm gonna deny it, since I don't know what you're talking about. I'm guilty of some lustful thoughts," he said, and saw her eyebrows go up. "Yeah, I admit it. Though it's not like that wasn't obvious. I'll also admit to being pissed off that a guy could leave you with the notion that sex is nothing but a big disappointment."

She just sat there, staring at him as if he'd dumped a pail of cold water over her head. Then she blinked. "Lustful thoughts?"

This woman was going to make him crazy. How had he thought for a second that he could read her? She looked surprised and sounded a little excited. Neither reaction made sense. "I promised you I'd be a gentleman and I aim to keep that promise."

Her gaze lowered to her cup, and then she drained the whiskey.

"Can I ask you a question?"

She seemed uncertain but nodded.

"Why do you think you're bad at social interaction?"

"I don't just think it." She shrugged. "It's true. All through school I was the shy younger kid who no one wanted to hang out with. I wasn't invited to parties or asked out on dates.

Which was fine with me because I spent a lot of time at my computer."

"Don't tell me you were one of those wonder kids who graduated from high school at thirteen."

"I was fifteen."

He'd been joking. Obviously she wasn't. "And college?"

"Eighteen," she said with a trace of apology. "But I stayed on for postgraduate studies, if that counts."

"I bet you've got a bunch of fancy letters after your name."

Shea smiled and shrugged.

Something else occurred to him. "Hey, should I be calling you Dr. Monroe?"

She rolled her eyes. "That would be my father. I haven't gotten my Ph.D. yet. I got bored with school."

Well, that explained a few things. He'd started to wonder if she'd been brought up in a convent. "So, is your father famous?"

"In the world of physics, yes, he's quite well-known."

"And your mother? She must be working on curing cancer."

Shea let out a startled laugh. "No, she's working on her fourth husband."

"Ah." Jesse held up the bottle in offering.

"Just a little," she said and leaned over with her cup out.

He poured them each a shot. "They divorce when you were young?"

"Ten. I left for boarding school soon after so it didn't matter."

Of course it mattered, he thought, but didn't say so. He watched her take a cautious sip while he tried to figure out what to say that wouldn't send the conversation downhill.

"My mother was a cocktail waitress Dad met while he was at a conference in Las Vegas. They never should've gotten married. Probably the stupidest and most impulsive thing my father ever did in his life."

"I don't know about stupid. They had you."

She bowed her head, a faint smile tugging at her lips as she studied the inside of her cup. "Tell me something about you."

Jesse snorted. "Hey, you know, I'm just a cowboy. What's there to tell?"

"You're also a pilot."

"Nowadays lots of ranchers have small planes or helicopters. It makes sense." Somehow he sensed her disappointment, which he didn't understand. She already knew he wasn't a rocket scientist or an Ivy League graduate.

"I know you spent time in the air force. Annie told me," Shea said, then quickly added, "I'm not sure how it came up, but we weren't gossiping."

"What else did she say about me?" he asked calmly, annoyed that he'd bothered because he wouldn't like the answer.

"She thinks you're terrific." Shea paused, a blush spreading across her cheeks. "I do, too."

Generally he wasn't much of a talker, but it'd never had anything to do with being at a loss for words. Damned if she hadn't made him tongue-tied. He had some mental adjustments to make. Missing pieces of the puzzle were falling into place for him. He hadn't been too far off base thinking she'd grown up sheltered. Wasn't a stretch for her to feel self-conscious about sex or how others perceived her.

"See, I probably shouldn't have said that," she murmured, nibbling at her lip and averting her eyes. "Told you I was bad at this stuff."

"Enough."

Her gaze shot back to his face. "What?"

"If you don't want pity, then quit feeling sorry for yourself. Or worrying about meeting other people's expectations. You have a good heart, Shea. You're smart and pretty and obviously strong-willed. That puts you way ahead of the curve. Nobody needs to throw you a pity party."

She seemed stunned. Her mouth opened, and she looked as if she might argue.

He leaned closer to her and lowered his voice. "I promised you I'd be a gentleman, but if you talk trash again I might have to kiss you to shut you up."

She shivered a little and said, "Yes, please."

12

"SHEA..." HE DRAWLED her name into a warning. His tone indicated he was done playing cat and mouse.

"I know what I said, Jesse. I'm not a child. I want you to—" Damn her voice for cracking. "I want it," she said softly, then in spite of ordering herself not to, added, "But only if you do."

"You know what I want," he said, his voice dipping into a husky murmur in the dim room. "But I also want you to be sure."

Briefly closing her eyes, she summoned all her courage and pushed to her feet. "Would you mind standing, please?"

He was confused. She saw it in his eyes, in the slight parting of his mouth, but he did as she asked. "Let me get rid of this," he said, glancing around for a place to set down the bottle.

"No, I might need another drink."

"If it takes alcohol to do whatever it is you intend doing, then you best rethink your plan."

She let out a nervous laugh. That was such a Jesse thing to say. He was still trying to protect her. This was a man who flew in horrible weather to rescue animals, a man who loved his home and family, and had been willing to risk his own safety to help a stranger. She'd only known him for what… three days? And yet she trusted him, she realized.

"You're right, no whiskey. I'll admit I'm nervous," she said, moving closer to him. "As if you couldn't tell, anyway." His faint smile warmed her. "I was wondering if maybe we could pick up where we left off…." She sucked in a deep breath. "You know, from earlier."

"I'm getting the idea," he said, shrugging out of his jacket and tossing it toward the cot, his gaze leveled on her face.

She tentatively put a hand on his chest, feeling the soft flannel against her palm, the hardness of muscle beneath the fabric. His breath ruffled her hair and she could smell the whiskey he'd drunk.

She tilted her head back to look into his eyes. No longer the warm chocolate-brown, they were darker now, almost black. He hadn't put his hands on her yet and a prick of impatience made her lower her lashes.

He caught her chin, and cut off her sigh with a soft kiss. Nothing more than a brief meeting of lips before he lifted his head.

"You can touch me, Shea. Anywhere you want," he murmured, and brushed her bangs to the side.

"I w-want t-to unbutton your shirt." She'd never stammered in her life. God, why now? "If it's okay."

"Anything you want to do is fine with me."

Straightening her spine, she unfastened the first button. "Oh." He was wearing thermals. Of course…what did she expect?

Jesse chuckled. "Winter's a bitch."

She made a low whimpering sound of agreement totally unfamiliar to her ears.

"Here." He took over the unbuttoning, discarded the shirt, then pulled off the beige thermal top and dropped it on the bench.

Shea could only stare in awe at his naked well-defined chest. Brian sure didn't have a chest like that. No man she knew had a chest like Jesse's. A minute ago she'd worried he'd be too cold without his shirt. Now she didn't care. No way he was taking that view away from her.

She quickly met his eyes, hoping she hadn't said anything out loud. From spending so much time alone, she had a bad habit of talking to herself.

"Everything all right?" he asked, picking up her hand and returning it to his chest.

"Fine. Terrific." She slowly slid her palm over the contour of his left pectoral muscle and let her fingers trail through the smattering of soft crisp hair tapering down to his flat stomach and disappearing into the waistband of his jeans.

"You want to take anything off?" he whispered, cupping her chin in one of his slightly rough hands and bringing her face up to meet his gaze.

"Of me?"

He smiled and kissed her forehead. "That's kind of what I had in mind, but you're calling the shots."

"So I could have you totally naked, but leave all my clothes on?" She was proud of herself for keeping a straight face.

"Um, if you really wanted," he said with so much reluctance that she broke down and laughed. One of his eyebrows went up in mock annoyance. "You sure you wanna mess with me?" he said, reaching around to cup her backside with both hands.

She gasped, still laughing as she flattened both palms on his chest. But he'd already pulled her body snugly against his, and he no longer looked amused. More determined.

"I'd prefer your clothes off but I can work with this," he whispered, and slid a hand inside her panties.

Standing as still as a statue, she forgot to breathe when he moved his hand to the front and cupped her sex. Smoothly he slid a finger inside, easing back when she instinctively tried to evade him.

"You feel good," he murmured, his raspy breath tickling her skin. "You're wet."

God, she was, and hot, almost feverish. She had this incredible urge to reach inside his jeans, to pull them off, see what he looked like completely naked. When was the last time she'd felt this heated rush? Maybe never.

He slid his finger back inside, and she started to tremble. "You okay?"

She nodded, leaving her face buried against his shoulder but moving her hips just enough to let him know what she wanted. It was crazy, this thrumming between her thighs. He'd hardly touched her, yet she could swear she was almost ready to explode. It wasn't possible.

"Kiss me," Jesse said, continuing to stroke her, lightly, relentlessly.

It wasn't easy lifting her head. Her weakened knees were barely keeping her upright. With his other arm sure and steady around her waist, she leaned back to look up at him. His face was hazy.

"Kiss me," he repeated, lowering his head so she could reach his mouth.

She brushed her upper lip along his lower one, and lightly scraped her teeth across his chin stubble. The rasp of the slight friction sent a tingle of excitement down her spine and, on impulse, she gently bit his lip.

A low moaning sound came from in his throat and he slanted his mouth over hers. He pushed his tongue inside and drove his finger in deeper while his thumb rubbed the sensitive nub that had her arching against his hand.

The feverish sensation again swept her perilously close to oblivion and with it came a wave of panic. "Oh, God," she said, as she tore her mouth away from his and shoved at his shoulder. "I can't stand it."

"Yes, you can," he murmured. "Let go."

"I can't… Oh, no—"

It was too late.

She froze, shocked at the fierceness of the spasm that jolted her. He kept moving his finger, coaxing yet another wave of sheer pleasure to shimmer through her body. It wouldn't stop. The waves kept coming, making her dizzy, confusing her, zapping her of energy until she started to collapse.

Jesse swept her up in his arms and cradled her to his chest. He carried her to the sleeping bag and gently lowered her to the blanket. It was startling to realize that she still wore most of her clothes. After what had just happened…God.

In a daze, she watched him cross the small room. When he reached down for his jacket, she saw muscles ripple across his shoulders and decided that she liked his back almost as much as his chest. He turned around and her gaze drew straight to his bulging fly.

Wow.

Bunching his jacket, he knelt on one knee beside her. Then he lifted her head and slid the makeshift pillow underneath. The sexy smile he gave her started another flutter low in her belly. Not possible. Couldn't be. Maybe it was hunger she felt.

"You still cold?" he asked, finger-combing the strands of hair clinging to her cheek.

"I don't think so."

"You're shivering," he said, stretching out on his side next to her and bracing his head in his hand.

"But not from the cold." She bit her lip. "You surprised me. I didn't—you went out of order," she said, her accusing tone bringing a glint of amusement to his eyes.

"Ah." His lips twitched. "You wanted me to undress you first."

"Yes. No." She sighed. "You confuse me."

"That makes two of us, darlin'." With a laugh, he started unbuttoning her shirt, then groaned when he got to the next layer. "Damn thermals."

Shea grinned. "You know I have no sympathy for you, right?"

He abruptly sat up and pulled her to a sitting position with him. Grabbing the hem, he yanked the top over her head and tossed it toward the stool.

She lost the smile, feeling vulnerable in her plain white bra. "What if this turns out bad?" she asked. "It could ruin everything between us."

"Have I disappointed you yet?"

"God, no." There was no point in being coy, but she blushed, anyway. "I think you already know that."

His gaze ran down to her breasts and then he splayed a hand across her belly. "We don't have to do this."

"What? No. I want to..." She almost laughed. "We kind of already have."

"We're barely warmed up." He pressed a kiss to her lips, and had her bra unhooked before she knew it.

She swallowed convulsively as he pulled the cups away from her breasts and touched her tightened nipples. Her chest heaved and nothing could stop her from shivering all the way down to her toes. He tore his gaze away from her breasts and met her eyes.

"Will you take off your jeans?" she asked, feeling a bit bashful sitting only in her panties.

He got to his feet, unsnapped, unzipped and stripped down to his boxers in one fluid motion. After gauging her for a moment, he pulled down the boxers, too.

The lantern hung on the other side of the stove at his back and provided only murky light. Any disappointment she experienced was due to her inability to see him as clearly as she'd like. She held her breath and waited for his next move. It didn't surprise her when he lowered himself to stretch out beside her again.

"You want to get under the blanket?" he asked, pushing her hair off her shoulder and nuzzling the side of her neck. "Or are you going to let me look at you for a while?"

She instinctively shrunk from his touch as if trying to preserve some distance between them. Oddly, though, that wasn't what she really wanted. Mostly she didn't want to have to answer his question.

He leaned back, a lazy smile teasing his lips, then casually cupped one of her breasts.

She trembled with want. "It's your—" She vaguely motioned at her own face. "I've never felt a man's beard on my skin before."

He rubbed his jaw and winced. "I'm sorry."

"No, it doesn't feel bad." She touched the cleft in his chin, gliding her finger over the shallow dimple, amazed she could have a heated reaction to the simple contact.

"I'll be careful." He went back to gently kneading her breast, then bent over her, kissing her slow and deep while his hand moved to her panties. He pulled them down her thighs, and she helped by bringing up her knees, and between the two of them, the panties ended up somewhere close to the stove.

Jesse slipped an arm behind her and laid her back down on the blanket and sleeping bag. His gaze ran down her body. "You're perfect."

"Stop it."

"What?" He skimmed his hand down the same path his gaze had taken. "To me, you are. You have the perfect size breasts," he said, pausing to cup the weight of her left one. "Perfect size and color nipples." He thumbed the hard nub, arousing it to an even stiffer peak than she'd thought possible.

She waited, breath held to see where he'd go next, but he

couldn't seem to get his fill of her breasts. He lowered his head and rolled his tongue over the sensitive tip before sucking it into his mouth. He was a little more forceful than she'd expected, and even more to her amazement it felt so good she didn't want him to stop.

He didn't just use his tongue, but also his teeth and firmed lips to tug and pull until she trembled again. "Too hard?" he asked, pressing soft soothing kisses there.

She shook her head. Obviously he couldn't see her response and drew back to look at her. In the soft glow of the lantern, his mouth was damp, the light sheen oddly seductive. "No, you did it—" she had to swallow "—you did it just right."

With a faint smile he administered the same treatment to her other breast. His hand had already moved down to her belly and the way he was positioned, she could feel his erection nudging her thigh.

"Jesse?"

His fingers leisurely traced her rib cage and he didn't seem in any hurry to stop. Laving her nipple a final time, he looked up.

"You said I could touch you," she said, not bothering to mask her impatience.

"I did." He rolled onto his back, clasping his hands behind his head. "I'm all yours."

She thought she knew exactly where she wanted to start, that is until she saw his muscled biceps flex into a solid mound of taut flesh. Lying there like that, his flat belly defined with narrow ridges of muscle, he looked like a centerfold in a woman's magazine.

When her gaze got to his waist, her breath caught painfully in her chest. God, he was hard. And thick. And it wasn't her imagination that heat actually radiated from him. To prove it to herself, she touched his erection. He inhaled sharply and pulsed against her palm. That didn't stop her. She wrapped her fingers around him and stroked up toward the smooth silky crown.

"You're killing me," he whispered in a hoarse voice.

"I am?" she said absently, astonished at how his penis jerked at even the slightest touch.

Physically speaking she was terrifically out of his league. She'd always been on the thin side. When she was in the middle of a project she often forgot to eat.

But Jesse…he was amazing. He really was perfect, she thought, sighing.

"Are you done yet?" he asked tightly.

"I'm just getting started…oh. What are you—"

He curled up and caught her left nipple between his teeth. She leaned into him, watching her nipple disappear into his mouth. He suckled her hard, then soft and slow, flicking his tongue over the pearled tip. When he withdrew it was to blow on the damp area, which created a delicious sensation in the cool air.

"I'm not finished," she said, startled to discover that she'd released him and he was moving away from her.

"I have to get my Levi's."

"No." She watched in dismay as he stood. "Why would…" Her objection trailed off when she got a glimpse of his naked butt, smooth and hard with muscle that flexed and released with each step he took. The light was frustratingly dim and she vaguely wondered if he'd care if she used the flashlight on him.

"Condoms," he said. "They're in my wallet."

It took a few seconds for his words to sink in. She felt instant shame. Protection wasn't something she would typically forget about. Although in her defense, she'd never been in a situation even close to this before. She'd had sex with exactly two different men and each time there'd been a mile of warning.

He found what he was looking for and dropped the jeans unceremoniously on the floor. It made her laugh. Even the thrill of watching him walk back to her fully aroused wasn't enough to curtail the nervous giggling.

"Trying to give me a complex?" He crouched next to her and straightened the sleeping bag and blanket around her bottom, startling her when he squeezed her left buttock. "What's so funny?"

"Nothing."

"Fine, but I'm sending you my therapy bill."

Shea sighed. "I'm nervous, okay?"

"Why?" He sat beside her, facing the opposite direction, his bare thigh flush with hers. "Why do I make you nervous?" he asked, in a low soothing murmur as he cupped her face in his hand.

She met his warm gaze. "It's not you, it's me."

He kissed the tip of her nose, brushed her lips with his, moved his hand to her breast. "What can I do to make it better?"

"I think you're already doing it," she said in a breathless rush, arching slightly and pushing herself into his palm.

He was a big man with big hands yet he handled her with the utmost care as he lightly kneaded, swirling a thumb around her tight nipple.

"You look dark and dangerous with all that beard stubble," she said, unexpectedly shivering as she placed her hand on his thigh.

"Ah." His mouth lifted with amusement. "You're one of those girls who likes a bad boy."

She gave an earnest shake of her head. "I like you, Jesse," she said and watched the humor fade from his face. Silence stretched for a long uncomfortable moment and her chest tightened with uncertainty. Had she said something wrong?

He tore open the packet he'd gotten from his wallet, and

donned the condom with a swift practiced motion. Then he took her arms and pulled them around his neck and kissed her, his tongue probing and determined until her misgiving vanished.

Unclenching her thighs, she parted them for him. He knelt between her legs, lifted the right one to his lips and kissed the inside of her ankle. Then moved to her calf, trailing hot kisses and warm moist breath all the way to the sensitive skin of her inner thigh.

Shea didn't think it was possible she could climax without him touching her more intimately, but she wouldn't rule it out, either. A mass of odd sensations pricked her feverish flesh. Longing burned deep inside her chest, so deep it was a place she hadn't known existed.

The frightened part of her wanted him to stop, the newly awakened feminine part of her wanted the moment to last forever. It wouldn't, though.

She felt the tension in his body as he moved over her and braced his hands on either side of her shoulders, felt the tremor in his arms as he held himself in check. Maybe it was contagious because Shea herself tensed. For her, it was anticipating the invasion of her body. It had been a long time for her, many months before Brian had finally moved out. And the experience hadn't been particularly pleasant.

But this wasn't Brian. This was Jesse—kind, sweet and hot-as-hell Jesse—who was making her feel things she hadn't known were possible. There was nothing indifferent about the way she wanted him right now.

He murmured a soft reassurance and then guided himself to her opening. Pausing, he used his fingers first, sliding them in to find her slick and ready. Lowering his head, he kissed her trembling lips, the kiss so full of passion that it took a second for her to realize he was pushing into her body.

Slowly at first, deep, harder, then deeper until she quivered helplessly beneath him.

He withdrew, though not all the way, and when she whimpered in protest, he moaned and thrust so deep she cried out his name.

13

JESSE'S ENTIRE BODY was trembling with the need for release. He normally had better self-control. This was messed up, acting like a horny seventeen-year-old. Dammit, he'd wanted this to be really special for her, but he fit too well. He knew she wasn't a liar, otherwise he might've suspected she was a virgin after all. She was that tight.

Only one thing to do. Withdraw. Even if it killed him. Which it just might.

He eased back, slowly sliding out of her, and then she made that soft helpless whimpering sound that tore at his heart. The kind of weak mewing that made him want to cut off his right arm rather than refuse her anything.

Against his better judgment, he pushed himself back inside and her wet, slick muscles clutched his cock, testing every last shred of his restraint. At this rate he wouldn't be able to hold off another minute.

He braced his hand on the side of her head and arched back to look at her flushed face. The shadowy light wasn't helping. He wanted to see the smoky gray-blue of her eyes, the rosy shade of her aroused nipples. Wanted to taste them again.

Shea's exasperation came out in a cute growl, and then she

locked her legs around his ass and lifted her hips. Her unexpected forcefulness reignited the fire in his veins.

The hell with it. He had a second condom. Next time… later he'd make it better for her. He rocked against her, slowly, letting her get used to him again, then he unlocked her legs, pushed them farther apart and thrust in deeper, harder, faster, until he was completely inside her. She started to squirm, caught his arm and dug into his flesh with her short nails.

He couldn't take any more. Couldn't hold off…

Jesse barely moved but came so violently he let out a cry that echoed in the small shack. Tremors racked his entire body and he felt so weak he didn't think his arms could hold him up. Afraid he'd crush her, he fell to the side, managing to hook an arm around her and take her with him.

Letting out a whoosh, she lay sprawled on top of him. "You're on the bare floor," she said, wiggling in an effort to break free.

"I don't care." His voice was a breathless rasp. "Stay with me."

"But, Jesse—"

"Shh." He pushed her hair back but it fell forward again, getting caught in his stubble-roughened jaw.

She shook it out of her eyes, and he tucked the loose tendrils behind her ear. Sighing, she quit fidgeting and lay there on top of him, her belly pressed close, her small, firm breasts hitting him right below his rib cage. She wasn't very tall, while he was six-two, and if she weighed more than a hundred and ten pounds he'd be shocked.

Without moving her bottom half, she stacked her palms on his chest, rested her chin on the back of her hands and stared at him.

"You okay?' he asked, unable to keep from touching her cheek.

At the slow heartfelt smile that curved her lips, a sense of bone-deep satisfaction filled his chest. "Wow."

He grinned and wondered if she could feel his ego expand through his pores. "Not disappointed?"

"Um, that was…" She moistened her lips. "Wow. That's all I can think of."

"All right." He ran his hand down her back, skimmed his palm over her nice round ass. Not too slim there. Perfect. "Now you're making fun of me."

"I am not." She turned her face, and like a contented kitten, rubbed her cheek against his chest hair. "You've changed my mind. I finally understand the big deal about sex."

"No, you don't," he said. "Not yet."

Her head came up, her eyes confused. "But I even—" She bit her lip, her gaze briefly flickering away.

"Because you came once?"

"Well, yes…" She stared at him now. Apparently he'd sparked her interest. "It was all pretty amazing."

His cock stirred, which was also pretty amazing. "If I'd lasted longer you could've had another orgasm."

She seemed skeptical, or maybe he was misreading her expression because the light sucked. Or maybe the frank talk was making her uncomfortable.

"I was worked up but I swear I won't be so quick on the draw next time. That's all I'm saying." He threaded his fingers through her hair, cupped her nape, holding her still while he lifted his head to kiss her.

She didn't seem nearly as willing as he'd hoped. Her mouth softened briefly but then she pulled back. "I don't understand why you're qualifying what happened. It was wonderful. More than I ever—" Her shoulders moved in a tiny shrug. "It was the first time for me."

Jesus, he really wanted to slam a fist into that Brian guy. Selfish bastard. Jesse snorted. He'd been a little bit of a pig himself. But he'd make it up to her. While he'd let silence lapse something registered.

Was Shea really as naive as he was beginning to think? He replayed their earlier conversation. She'd lived a fairly sheltered life. He couldn't ignore the possibility that she didn't understand there was more than one kind of orgasm.

"I only have one condom left," he said, more regretful than she'd ever guess. "But we can be creative until we get back to the Sundance."

Her eyes widened slightly and a smiled tugged at her lips. "Tonight? We get to do it again?"

Jesse laughed and hugged her tighter. "Oh, yeah, we're gonna do it again."

"WOW." SHEA LET her head drop back on Jesse's bunched jacket. Beneath her the blanket and sleeping bag were twisted together in a tangled heap.

Jesse flopped onto his back next to her, panting as if he'd run a marathon. The woman was going to kill him. He was too old to go this many rounds. For the past four hours they'd either been making love, resting from making love or about to make love. And yet he'd managed to hold off using the second condom. Damn, she was a quick study.

"Come here." She'd rolled to her side and was smoothing out the blanket.

"Hell, no. I'm keeping my distance. You're gonna give me a heart attack and we can't even call 911."

She giggled. "I didn't mean I wanted to do anything, I need the rest, too. I only wanted to share the blanket with you."

The wooden planks were cold and rough under his back, and he could see their breath in the chilly air. "I have to go throw another log on the fire."

"I'll do it." She jumped up before he could object.

The slight sway of her naked hips as she approached the

log pile made him glad he hadn't hastily gotten up to help her. Instead, he clasped his hands behind his head and enjoyed the view.

She glanced back at him. "You could be straightening out the sleeping bag."

"I could."

"You're making me self-conscious."

Jesse chuckled. After what they'd been doing? "Seriously?"

Groaning, she gave her hair a toss and then opened the stove door and carefully arranged a log. "We're getting low on wood."

"Good thing we've been using body heat." His view temporarily obstructed, he rose to a crouch and shook out their makeshift mattress.

Then he stayed still, listening to what was happening outside. The wind hadn't picked up again, so that was good. Last he'd looked the snow had subsided, as well.

"I should check on Candy Cane," Shea said, on her way toward the door.

"Let me." He was on his feet, his arm around her waist pulling her naked body to his before she could protest.

"We have to stop this," she murmured against his mouth, then parted her lips for his tongue, looping her arms around his neck.

He kissed her soundly while filling his hands with her soft round ass. "You mind checking the lantern while I look outside?"

"Of course not. If nothing else, we have a lot of fuel. Probably wasn't a good idea to leave that much around but I'm glad for the light."

"Me, too." Before he released her, his gaze dropped to her flushed nipples. They seemed to get rosier the more aroused she became. He dipped his head for a taste.

She shivered in his arms. "You said we were giving it a rest."

"We are." He rolled his tongue over one stiff peak. "This is nothing," he murmured before sucking it into his mouth.

"You're crazy," she whispered, arching closer.

He couldn't disagree. Something about her inexperience and eager curiosity turned him on like no other woman ever had. Not just that, but the smell and taste of her, the candid questions and unguarded responses to his touch, made him throb with a longing that he refused to examine too closely.

Sex had never altered the way he thought about a woman afterward. Maybe in high school, when he was sixteen and thinking with his dick too much… In one year he could've sworn he'd fallen in love twice. Which wasn't implying that love had anything to do with Shea and him. But he couldn't deny being with her felt different.

All she had to do was say wow, which she'd said ungodly often, and he'd start getting hard all over again. Jesus. What was up with that?

He switched to her other breast and flicked his tongue over her extended nipple. Her answering moan almost had him rethinking the whole let's-give-it-a-rest thing, but he saw the mark his stubbled chin had left on her shoulder. He indulged in a final roll of his tongue over the tight nub then kissed the small whisker burn.

Dammit, he'd tried to be so careful.

She blinked drowsily at him. "What's wrong?"

"Nothing. Get under the blanket. I'll be right back." He rubbed her firm backside, then quickly let her go before his good intentions evaporated.

He'd have to give it up and use the condom soon. That was the problem. He'd already come twice, but only once inside her. And damn but he wanted to see the wonder in her face when she climaxed with him buried deep in her tight, wet sex.

Hell, he had to put on the brakes, remember that they had all night. Or the rescue team would end up finding them in a coma. He was pretty sure Shea wouldn't appreciate making headlines in the *Salina Gazette.*

Letting in some cold was inevitable, but he opened the door as little as possible and the mare looked up at him with mild interest. She was a Safe Haven rescue. In all likelihood the poor animal had been through a lot worse than waiting out a storm under the eaves of a line shack. "You doing okay, girl?"

She snorted steam then turned at the noise that came from a clump of snow sliding off the branch of a spruce.

It was dark but the sky was no longer blotted out by eerie purplish-gray clouds swollen with snow. Overhead he could see the soft glow of the quarter moon struggling to shine through. Good sign. Dawn wouldn't come for another seven hours. By then he expected the weather would be clear and the terrain negotiable. If not for their dwindling log supply and lack of condoms, he'd have mixed feeling about being able to leave.

"Jesse?" She sounded anxious.

He closed the door. "Yeah, sweetheart?" He turned to her but stopped in his tracks. He wasn't the type to use endearments, certainly not unconsciously. Clearing his throat, he joined her on the sleeping bag. "Nothing's wrong. I was just looking at the sky."

She yawned and quickly covered her mouth. "Good news, I hope."

"Looks clear. I think the storm is over." He stretched out beside her and brought her to his chest.

She pressed her cheek against his skin. "You're cold."

"Ah, sorry."

"No, stay where you are." She clutched his shoulder. Her palm was warm from the fire and she rubbed it up and down his arm, pausing to mold her hand to the curve of his biceps.

"I like touching you," she whispered. "I want to feel every square inch of your body."

"Um, think you've already done that."

She laughed softly. "Oh, my. I believe you're right."

Jesse smiled and kissed her hair. She was so damn cute. "Did I miss anything on you?"

"Not even a freckle." She sighed, her breath warm and soothing on his chest. "I'm sore in very weird places. I'm not complaining, though." She snuggled closer. "It's just odd."

The way she spouted whatever was on her mind made him realize how much time he'd spent trying to decode other women. Shea still confused him, but it wasn't by acting coy or pretending to be someone she wasn't. "Another reason we need to cool it for a while."

She lifted her head and frowned at him. "How long?"

"Damn." He couldn't help laughing. "You're gonna kill me, woman."

Her mouth twisted in a wry smile. "I didn't mean it like that," she muttered shyly, then settled down again. "We should do some talking."

He hated the sound of that. "Sleep is what we need."

She nodded absently, lightly running her palm over his chest, waking his nipples. "I sort of feel sorry for Brian."

"Your ex-boyfriend?"

"Mmm-hmm."

Just what he wanted to do, talk about her ex. "Why?"

"He doesn't get it. He has no idea what he's missing out on. Maybe Serena can teach him a few tricks like you taught me. She's his new girlfriend."

Jesse tried not to laugh, but his body vibrated from the restraint, and she reared back to stare at him. "I have nothing to say to that," he muttered.

She sniffed. "I mean, how is a person supposed to know if someone doesn't show them?"

"Very good question," he said as seriously as he could, and coaxed her to lay her head down again.

"It's a valid point."

"I'm not arguing with you."

She sighed. "Can I tell you a secret?"

"Shoot."

"Everyone thinks I love my job just because I'm so good at it. And I do like the work. I love computers. It's very black-and-white. No judgment calls required. But I hate that everyone assumed that was the path I'd take. No one asked what I wanted to do. Not even my parents." She went very still. "Not even me, come to think of it."

"You just went with the flow."

"That's exactly what I did because I didn't know anything else." Her voice had dropped off as if the thought saddened her.

"That's not a bad thing being able to do what you like." He wasn't keen on following the conversation in the direction it was headed. His new crossroad wasn't up for discussion.

"I understand, I'm lucky in that respect. Because I despise change. Well, not so much anymore, I'm making progress. Only baby steps, but hey, I'm here. I didn't let my mom badger me into spending Christmas with her new family."

"Good for you." Jesse rubbed her back and thought about that first day he'd taken her on a ride up to the ridge. She'd barely said a few sentences. She was making up for it now. He didn't mind. As long as the subject stayed on her. "You work for a big company?"

She nodded. "Being a pilot you may have heard of them. Zigman Security Analysts."

"Yeah, I've heard of them." Jesus, heavy hitters. "They're involved in more than aviation. Don't they have a lot of government and military contracts?"

"They do, but I try to stay away from classified material. I have the necessary clearance so I'll get involved if it's a matter of national security, but I prefer to stay more autonomous."

Stunned by the new information, he stared down at her. She didn't look up to gauge his reaction. The woman clearly had some teeth in the world of high-tech security, but it was all in a day's work to her.

"I envy you, Jesse," she said softly. "You've been places, done amazing things, and given a choice, you've come back to do what you love."

"It's not that simple." He heard the quiet words come out of his mouth and couldn't believe he'd said them.

She looked up at him now. "What do you mean?"

He smiled. "Nothing," he said, picked up her hand and brought it to his lips. He kissed her palm, and then drew a finger into his mouth.

She met and held his gaze. "Is it about Afghanistan?"

Releasing her hand, he glanced away and rubbed his eyes. "I thought we were talking about you."

"I'm sorry. Annie told me you'd been deployed when you were in the air force. Nothing more was said." She paused. "No, that's a lie. Annie mentioned something about people thinking you weren't yourself. But that's all, I swear."

Coming from another woman he might've assumed she was fishing. But not Shea. Jesse thought for a moment about how much he wanted to reveal. "I know what folks think, Shea. They're wrong. Though I haven't found any need to correct them. Around here, once folks take something into their heads..." He shrugged.

"You don't think the war changed you?"

"I'm sure it has to some degree. Killing is an ugly and senseless business. Even if it's not in your face, you understand the reason why you're carrying a rifle real quick." He swallowed around the sudden lump in his throat. Calling back memories never turned out well. "It would be naive of me to think that my views and opinions haven't been altered. But basically I'm the same man who was shipped to boot camp."

"What are people seeing, Jesse? Do you think they assumed you'd changed because it was expected?" When he didn't answer, her body tensed against him. "I don't mean to pry. I really don't. I want to understand, but you don't have to tell me anything."

He hugged her, burying his face in her hair for a moment. It was crazy, his sudden yearning to unload. Why her? Sure, they didn't know each other well so she was safe. But so was Noah, he'd served in the army and had a much better understanding of what Jesse had gone through.

Except his restlessness had nothing to do with the air force or Afghanistan. And if he told her the truth, that he couldn't seem to find a place here anymore, that he felt irrelevant, she'd never understand. She might even think he was a stupid self-absorbed bastard who couldn't appreciate a family who loved him. That they cared deeply about him wasn't in question. He knew that. But it was hard to explain, this weird sense of not belonging anywhere.

Still, he didn't want to cut off Shea, let her think that tonight had been only about sex. He truly felt something for her. Couldn't name it precisely, but the fact was he'd been happier in the past twenty-four hours than he'd been in years.

He smiled. Ironic he'd finally found a slice of peace and contentment in this broken-down shack. He kissed her forehead, then the tip of her nose.

She eagerly offered him her lips.

He parted them with his tongue and thoroughly explored her mouth. She drew her hand down his belly, and he knew he could easily distract her if he wanted.

Instead he caught her wrist and forced her to retrace her

path up to his chest, then he kissed her palm. “First,” he said, taking a deep fortifying breath and praying he wouldn’t re-gret this, “we’re going to finish talking.”

14

SHEA FERVENTLY WISHED she could see his face more clearly in the obscured glow of the lantern. She knew when he smiled because of the flash of his white teeth, or when he stared at the ceiling. The way the light fell, he could probably see her a lot better, which was absolutely unfair since she had enough trouble picking up social cues. But there was one thing about which she was certain. He wasn't as tense as before. His body was more relaxed, his heartbeat no longer pounding against her ear.

"You get to choose the topic," she said, hoping to keep the mood nice and easy between them. He clearly didn't like talking about himself, and she didn't blame him a bit. She'd surprised herself at her own chattiness. Not like her at all.

"I'm going to tell you something that I want kept between us," he said, lightly squeezing her hand.

She nodded, then said, "All right," to make sure he knew she understood.

"If I've changed, it's not about the air force or going to Afghanistan. Joining the service turned out to be the right decision for me, even though me joining up was kind of expected. It's what McAllister men have done for generations.

Not Cole—turned out he was allergic to the uniform. It's kind of a funny story…maybe I'll tell you later….

"Anyway, I was a junior in college over in Billings when my father passed away. He'd been battling cancer for a year. We knew it was coming but I guess you're never really prepared."

"I'm sorry."

"Yeah, it was hard, especially for Mom and Rachel." He let out a short laugh. "Hell, it was tough on all of us. Cole had just turned twenty-one and being the eldest son the responsibility of the ranch was passed to him. Rachel and Trace were young, both of them still in high school. And Mom…" He shook his head. "She was so overcome with grief we didn't know what to do about her…. Good thing she had two teenagers who needed looking after.

"Of course, I came home as soon as I got the phone call. I was here most weekends, anyway—that's why I chose a college in Billings. After the funeral I told Mom and Cole I wasn't going back to school, that I'd drop out, stay and help run the Sundance. They wouldn't hear of it. Mom cried, said that's not what my father would've wanted. Cole got up in my face and accused me of not having faith in him to run things." Jesse inhaled a deep breath. "It wasn't like that…. I wanted to help, yet I'd never felt more helpless in my life."

Shea sensed his pain despite his modulated tone. He hadn't stopped stroking her back, and though it felt wonderful, she understood his need for the repetitive movement. "Cole was probably feeling helpless, too, don't you think? I mean twenty-one is still young to be handed so much responsibility. Just because I had a high IQ everyone seemed to think I was supposed to know everything. The expectations were unrealistic, but that didn't mean their disappointment didn't hurt."

"That must have been tough. What is your IQ, anyway?"

"Uh-uh." She never told anyone anymore. "We were talking about you."

"That high, huh?"

She gave his nipple a light twist, and he jumped. "What happened when you returned to school?"

"Nothing." He shoved her hand out of harm's way. "I managed to survive the semester. My grades slipped but I didn't care much."

"You were still grieving. Did you have someone there, a buddy or girlfriend?"

"Yeah, actually, I'd started going out with someone a few weeks before my dad passed away. Another student a year behind me. We met at a football game when I spilled my beer on her."

"Nice."

Jesse smiled. "Chelsea was great. Smart, good sense of humor. Got a job as a marketing rep in San Francisco after graduate school. Who knows where she is now."

"What happened? Were you ever serious?" Shea curbed her urge to pepper him with questions and let him answer without interruption. It wasn't easy, though.

"Honestly, I thought we were for a while, but she didn't like that I joined the air force. Initially I would've been out by the time she finished graduate school." He breathed in deeply. "I was in Afghanistan when I got her letter. Said she was moving on. I didn't blame her."

"I'm sorry." Shea wasn't curious about her anymore. She didn't like her, period.

"I didn't take it as hard as I should've, which meant she was right. There was no future for us."

"No, I can't see you living in San Francisco. I can't imagine you anywhere but here." Shea felt him tense.

He stopped rubbing her back and stretched both arms over

his head. "No more useless talk about the past," he said casually, but she wasn't fooled. Something was bothering him.

The thing was, she couldn't figure out what she'd said to cause him to withdraw. Was he thinking about his old girlfriend? Did he regret their breakup? What a depressing thought. "Have you talked to her since you were discharged?"

"Who?"

"Chelsea."

"Oh, no. There wasn't anything to say." He brought his arms back around Shea. "You want to talk about your old boyfriend?"

"No."

"Okay, then." He bit her earlobe, then dragged his lips down the side of her neck. "Enough talk. More action."

Shea tried to laugh it off, but his body had already coiled with a different kind of tension, and she lifted herself up to brace her hands against his shoulders and keep him at bay.

The move didn't stop him. He flipped her onto her back, grasped both her wrists in one hand and pulled them over her head, pinning them to the sleeping bag. She automatically arched her breasts against him.

"Talk about going from zero to sixty," she said, breathless, still appalled that she could be this quickly turned on. It felt like someone else's body, not hers.

"Complaining?" He bent his head to suck a nipple into his mouth and his free hand slipped between her thighs.

"What are you doing?" she asked.

He leisurely used his tongue to tease her already stiff nipple. "Really?" he asked with amusement as he moved to her other breast. "You need an explanation?"

She shuddered when his mouth made contact again. He had quite a tight hold of her wrists, and it was utterly shocking how much she liked it.

His fingers dipped into her folds and she could feel his arousal hot and pulsing against her outer thigh.

"You're using sex to shut me up," she said while she could still think.

He paused for a second. "Yes. Problem?"

Want and need burned low in her belly. "I can live with that," she murmured, then gasped when he pushed his finger in all the way.

JESSE WOKE WITH A cramp in his shoulder. He hated to move and risk disturbing Shea. She was still sound asleep, her warm soft body tucked against him, her tangled hair a quarter inch away from tickling his nose.

The lantern had burned down and he suspected they had little more than smoldering ashes left in the stove, but between the blanket and practically staying glued together they'd managed to keep sufficiently warm.

Stretching his neck to the side seemed to help relieve the kink in his shoulder. She didn't stir. She had to be exhausted. He sure as hell felt as if he'd been hauling hundred-pound hay bales. Generally he tried to keep himself in good shape but last night…

He shot a look at the door. It was morning. Still early, judging by the pinkish light seeping under the door. But if he didn't get up and use the radio soon, it wouldn't be long before Cole brought out the hounds. Jesse wouldn't blame him—if the situation were reversed, he'd have loaded the snowmobiles before first light.

Crap. That was exactly what Cole had done, he just knew it, and Jesse had damn well better be prepared for the cavalry to descend.

He tried to angle his arm on the off chance he'd be able to see his watch and not wake Shea. It was still too dark no matter how hard he squinted. Maybe he was wrong about the sun being up. He inhaled her sweet musky scent. They both smelled like sex. Yeah, he wouldn't mind being stranded for another day or so.

Of course that would leave too much time for more talking. He'd never been an open book, didn't see the need, and yet he'd told Shea so much. He wasn't sure why he'd let down his guard like that. Maybe because she'd be leaving soon.

No, it wasn't that. In her own way, Shea understood him more than almost anyone. Her questions might be blunt, but they were also right on point, and the woman didn't give an inch. Strange how much he liked that. Liked her. Which didn't change the fact that there was still no place for him here, and he still hadn't come up with a better solution than reenlisting.

He looked at her sleeping, so pretty and soft. He'd miss her.

The thought ate at him more than it should have. It was just sex, he reminded himself. For both of them. She was leaving two days after Christmas. Until then it would be fun. They'd spend time together. As long as he was on the ground, he'd probably go help out at Safe Haven.

If he was called away then…damn, the idea really sucked. Christmas was in what…three days? Last week he would've welcomed the excuse to get out of Blackfoot Falls. And now?

Shea moaned softly and rubbed her silky cheek against his shoulder.

He didn't move, waiting to see if she was awake or not. Her slow, even breath warmed his skin. She was still asleep, but he'd have to rouse her soon. Real soon, since he had no clue as to the time. He stretched out his neck again, relieving more of the pressure. What a dumbass. He should just get up. Check outside, check the fire. If he disturbed her, she'd go back to sleep.

"Jesse?" she murmured groggily, bringing a small fist up to her face.

He touched her hair. "Yeah?" he said, and felt her slow smile draw across his flesh.

"It wasn't a dream."

"What?"

"Us." She opened her hand and laid her palm on his chest. "Last night."

"Best dream I ever had if it was."

"You're sweet."

He grinned. "Think so? Even when I tell you we have to get up?"

She skimmed her hand to his belly. "You sure about that?"

Damned if his poor tired cock didn't twitch. "There's a term for women like you."

"I am not…" She lifted her head. "Okay, maybe a little. But only with you."

Oh, boy. He had to think about that one. Or maybe he shouldn't. He cleared his throat. "All kidding aside, I have to find out what time it is. We don't want to be caught with our pants down, so to speak."

She giggled, but quickly sobered. "No, that would be bad." She sat up and twisted toward the door.

More dawn light was seeping in. He vaguely considered how the door faced northeast, which meant the sun had to be pretty high, but he was more interested in the silhouette of her breasts now that he could see her more clearly. He traced her puckered nipple.

Shea froze. "Did you hear that? Sounded like a motor or engine."

Abruptly he pushed to his feet.

"Maybe it was my imagination."

He hadn't heard anything but he'd been preoccupied. "Stay here," he said, grabbing his Levi's and yanking them on, not bothering with underwear, thermals or the zipper.

At the door he stopped and listened. Still nothing. Maybe

it was the mare growing impatient. The second he opened the door he heard voices.

Shit.

Barefooted, bare-chested, he stepped outside and pulled the door closed behind him. Cole and Trace were approaching the shack. They stopped dead in their tracks and stared at him as if he'd grown a pair of horns.

"Everything okay?" Cole asked, frowning at the door, and then at Jesse's chest and feet.

"Fine. We're good." Jesse glanced past them at the snowmobiles they'd left parked near where the trail had been covered with snow. "Anybody else with you?"

Cole shook his head, his expression of confusion transforming into amusement.

"Stay here." Shivering from the frosty air, Jesse backed up. "Don't come inside."

Trace's face lit with a grin the size of the whole state of Montana. By the time Jesse opened the door a crack, his brother was laughing. "I'd expected you to be a little happier to see us."

Cursing under his breath, Jesse yanked the door closed again and pinned them with a warning glare. "Shut up," he said irritably. "Both of you."

Cole shrugged and drew his lips together in a tight line, but his shoulders started to shake with silent laughter.

Jesse swore again and entered the shack. Then he stuck his head outside one last time. "Dammit, I mean it."

AFTER SHEA DRIED her hair and pulled on thermals and the thickest sweater she owned, she lingered at her bedroom window holding open the curtain and staring outside. Snow blanketed the ranch and all the land up to the foothills where Jesse had taken her that second day. Sun, blue sky, such a beautiful, peaceful scene made it hard to believe a storm had blown through.

With little enthusiasm for going downstairs, she released the curtain and let it fall into place. The ride back with Cole and Trace had been embarrassing enough, now she had to face Mrs. McAllister, Rachel and Jamie.

Of course, Jesse's brothers had said nothing inappropriate. They'd seemed genuinely concerned about her welfare. But they had to know what had happened between her and Jesse. Well, not the details, or that the earth had actually moved last night, but in a general sense they knew something had changed.

Funny, a few days ago it wouldn't have crossed her mind that anyone would think anything of them spending the night together. But now…after what they'd shared…after how he'd learned her body better than she understood it herself…

God, already she missed him. Even the steaming hot shower she'd taken hadn't erased his smell from her skin. She wondered where he was at this very minute. Still in the shower? Taking a nap? In the kitchen drinking coffee?

Darn it, she'd have to leave her room to find out.

The women were in the kitchen when she went downstairs. She'd seen them briefly when she arrived and was instructed to head straight for the shower and warm clothes.

"What can I get you?" Mrs. McAllister asked the second she spotted Shea. "Coffee, hot chocolate, tea?"

Rachel stood at the stove, but at her mother's voice she abruptly turned, her anxious gaze sizing Shea up from head to toe. "I'm frying bacon, but we also have ham and sausage and the biscuits are in the oven. How do you like your eggs? I make a mean veggie-and-cheese omelet."

"For heaven's sake, would you let her answer me?" Mrs. McAllister pulled out a chair at the kitchen table. "I know you drink coffee but we're stocked with the aforementioned."

"Coffee sounds really good." Shea hesitated, eyeing the coffeemaker sitting to the right of the modern cook-top stove. Marked stainless-steel canisters of flour and sugar and platters of meat crowded the beautiful pearl-gray granite countertops. "I can pour it myself."

"So can I. Please sit."

Shea meekly did as she was told, murmuring, "Thank you, Mrs. McAllister."

"You have to call me Barbara. Everyone does." She looked pretty and youthful with her auburn hair pulled back into a French braid. Setting the steaming mug in front of Shea, she said, "You drink it black, right?"

She nodded. "Thank you." She glanced around and saw a couple of mugs sitting near the sink. Had Jesse come and gone already? "You have a beautiful kitchen. It's so big."

"It was remodeled five years ago." Barbara poured herself a cup and added cream. "The boys do a lot of the work themselves during winter months when they don't have as much to do outside." She took a seat at the table, her eyes troubled. "Are you sure you're all right?"

Rachel turned away from the stove to look at Shea.

"I'm fine. Though I was very lucky your son spotted me. I'm not sure I could've found my way back." She'd purposely not used his name and still she felt her cheeks heat.

Barbara studied her a moment. "As soon as we got the message that Jesse had collected you we all relaxed. We knew you were in good hands."

"But he had to land in a field of snow because of me. He could've been in danger and it would've been my fault. I'm so sorry." She stared down at her hands wrapped around the warm mug. "And Candy Cane, she had to—"

"She's nice and warm, happily munching hay in the barn," Barbara assured her. "I expect she was given some oats, too."

"And Annie." It suddenly hurt to breathe. Oh, God, Annie would never trust her again. "I need to call her right away."

"I already did." Rachel left the stove to pat Shea's shoulder. Barbara had her hand on Shea's arm. "Nobody is upset with you," Rachel said.

"Certainly not us, and not Annie. We're all relieved that you're both safe," Barbara added.

Shea breathed in deeply. It was still hard to look up. Weird having these strangers touching her, but she didn't mind as much as she normally would have. Maybe because she knew they genuinely cared and wanted nothing from her.

The stray thought unnerved her. She hadn't considered it before. But it was true…someone always seemed to want something from her.

For Brian it had been leverage within the company—she was their star and he'd ridden her coattails until he'd come into his own. Her boss fawned over her because she made him look good and earned him huge bonuses. And her parents… sometimes the knowledge that she was barely more than her father's prize pupil and her mother's sounding board did hurt a little. Time had made acceptance easier.

"Shea?" Barbara squeezed her arm. "Please believe that we aren't mad at you." She paused, then in a voice taut with concern, asked, "Are you hurt in some way? Is there something you're not telling us? We have a good doctor in town."

"No, I'm fine. Really. I was wondering if Annie's going to fire me."

Barbara sank back in her chair and smiled.

Rachel breathed a relieved sigh.

"No," both women said at the same time.

"I'd understand if she did." Shea brought the mug to her lips and drank deeply even though the brew was still hot. She felt chilled again, although the kitchen was nice and warm.

"Honey, don't be so hard on yourself," Barbara said. "I bet you'll feel better once you talk to Annie yourself, but first—"

The sizzling bacon popped and spit. Muttering a mild curse, Rachel rushed back to the stove.

"Nice language, young lady." Barbara eyed her daughter.

"You let the boys get away with it."

Barbara's lips lifted in a wry smile. "They usually have the good sense not to say it to my face."

"Trace? Good sense? Since when?"

Barbara sighed her disapproval loud enough for Rachel to hear, and winked at Shea. "How many brothers and sisters do you have?"

"None." That wasn't true. She always forgot about the new twins and Frankie. "I have half siblings, but they're young and I don't really know them." She took another sip. "I have three stepbrothers, as well," she said, and wished she hadn't. "I don't know them, either," she mumbled, annoyed with herself for awkwardly trying to fill the silence.

Rachel and Barbara were both lovely women. There was no reason to be uncomfortable around them. They hadn't treated her as if they suspected about her and Jesse last night.

"Speaking of brothers, where are those bums?" Rachel drew back the blue-checked curtains and peered out the window. "If they think I'm keeping breakfast warm for them they can—"

"Gee, cut us some slack." Cole walked through the door to the dining room, his dark hair damp and slicked back. "We were out being heroes this morning." He smiled at Shea and his mother, then sniffed the air. "Hmm, fresh biscuits."

"That's right." Trace walked in directly behind him. "Heroes," he said with a finger pointed at Rachel. "You got that?"

"Oh, shut it." Rachel transferred bacon from the pan to a platter. "Make more coffee while you're up."

"Ah, my loving brood. Brings a tear to a mother's eye."

Barbara picked up her mug and got to her feet. "Where's Jesse?"

"He went to the barn to check on the mare." Cole snatched a strip of bacon and just missed the wrath of Rachel's big black spatula. "He'll be here any second."

Jamie entered next. "Hi, Shea, you look better." She gave Shea's shoulder a reassuring rub as she passed.

"Mornin', Jamie." Trace flashed a megawatt smile.

"Forget it." She waved him off and sidled up to Cole. "Rachel told you to make the coffee."

Everyone but Trace and Shea laughed. Grumbling to no one in particular, Trace brought out a canister and filters from the upper cabinet.

Shea brought her coffee to her lips, apprehensive about Jesse's eventual appearance and wishing she could hide behind the large blue ceramic mug. Everyone was being great. No sly or questioning looks, but did they all have to be here at the same time? Jeez, she was suddenly feeling claustrophobic. Bad enough she'd already counted all the cabinets in threes.

Scanning the pale yellow wall decorated with copper molds, she saw the clock and was shocked to see it was only ten-fifteen. It felt like four in the afternoon. She had to think of an excuse to leave. She couldn't be rude—these people had been inconvenienced because of her, yet they remained so gracious. They were all talking, laughing, teasing each other with a familiarity that frightened her. She didn't belong here. Even if she wished she could.

She drew in a deep breath, let it out slowly, then silently cleared her throat. "I'd feel better if I spoke to Annie myself, so if you don't mind…" She stood and moved back, wincing when her chair scraped the wood floor.

More than her timid voice, the horrible noise caught everyone's attention. All eyes were on her and she wanted to die. Right here, right now. She wished Jesse had never found her out in the storm.

"You need to eat first."

At his voice she jumped. Jesse had come through the same door as everyone else but he'd hung back, out of her peripheral vision, and was watching her with a cool detachment that pierced her heart.

"Is Candy Cane all right?" she asked, fearing that's what had him acting strangely.

"The mare is fine."

"Oh. Good." She swallowed. Maybe he was just tired. Or perhaps he wanted to make it clear that last night was last night and now everything would revert to normal between them.

She glanced at the table, her abandoned chair. Her purse… it was still at Safe Haven. "I don't have a phone."

He turned away to get a mug out of the cabinet. "You can use the landline in the den," he said, crossing to the coffeemaker and finding the carafe nearly empty.

"I'm working on that," Trace said. "Take mine."

It was quiet, way too quiet. Thankfully only for a few seconds and then everyone got busy with what they'd been doing.

Shea stared down at her trembling hand. Dammit, dammit, dammit. She didn't know where the den was, but she didn't trust her voice to ask. She set down her mug, made fists and shoved them into her pockets. At least no one was looking at her, not even Jesse.

"Wait," he said, just as she was about to leave the kitchen.

She already had one foot on the threshold. Easy to pretend she hadn't heard him and keep moving.

He took the decision out of her hands by catching her arm and startling her to death. He had to have flown across the kitchen. She met his gaze, then looked past him. The others were being careful to pay them no attention.

"It's okay," he whispered. "You call Annie, and then we'll eat." Without checking to see if anyone was watching, he slid an arm around her shoulders and hugged her close as he walked with her. "Don't wait breakfast on us," he called to no one in particular. "We'll eat in a little while."

15

SHEA CLIMBED INTO the warmth of Jesse's big pickup, exhausted from working half a day at Safe Haven. Everyone, including Annie, had urged her not to come in after the overnight ordeal, but she couldn't postpone seeing Annie. She'd dreaded facing the woman who'd trusted her, the woman whom Shea had failed.

In the end it'd been easier than expected but still hard. Probably because Annie had been so kind. She'd hugged Shea, told her three times how glad she was that she was safe, and no, she didn't blame her at all because Annie had made a lousy call in letting her go after Caleb. They finally had to make a pact not to beat themselves up anymore.

The biggest disappointment of the day was there'd been no sign of Caleb. Everyone told Shea not to worry about him. She did anyway.

At least Candy Cane was fine, stuffed with oats, warm and happy. Jesse had arranged for the mare's return to Safe Haven and for Shea's rental to be driven to the Sundance so she could ride back with him. The hay Shea had ordered from the hardware store had been delivered and unloaded, and seeing the relief on Annie's face had done Shea's heart good.

Jesse reversed the truck and as he steered them toward the

drive, Shea twisted around to give Annie and two of the volunteers a final goodbye. It wasn't as if she wouldn't see them tomorrow, but she was still overcome with gratitude and a bunch of weird fuzzy emotions that had her thinking askew.

Annie grinned and gave her a thumbs-up.

Shea promptly turned back to face the dashboard. A week ago she wouldn't have known what the gesture meant. It was about Jesse. No doubt in her mind.

"They're gossiping about us," she said to him, "you know that, right?"

"'Course they are." He chuckled, then glanced over at her with a look of concern. "Does that bother you?"

She stared down at his hand closed over hers resting on the seat between them. "I work in the same office as a guy who dumped me. If I ever was squeamish about gossip I'd be over it by now."

"That's the spirit."

Jeez, maybe she was schizophrenic. Now that was a comforting thought, especially since Jesse eyed her as if he'd considered the same possibility.

"I don't know what happened this morning or why I acted the way I did," she said, releasing his hand and wrapping her arms around herself. They'd been busy, and he hadn't pushed, so she'd managed to avoid the topic. Now she wished the conversation was over. "Your mom, Rachel, everyone was so nice to me. But I just don't think I can face them tonight. Darn it, I'm sleeping in the barn."

"You're sleeping with me." He put both hands on the wheel to navigate a curve.

"Jesse…"

"What?"

"I'm not sure that's a good idea," she said, but inside she was excited that he still wanted her.

"So you are afraid of people talking."

"No, not really. Most of that stuff goes over my head. But it's your family. They love you so much and I don't want to say anything stupid or wrong."

He seemed to tense. The road had straightened. He could've taken her hand again but he didn't.

She studied his profile and wondered which part of that he objected to. "I don't know why I'm so weird or why I clam up the way I do. But it's been this way forever. I can't explain it."

"You're not weird." He found her hand again and squeezed it. "They mean well, but my family can be a little overwhelming. And when Trace and Rachel get into it…man, you'd think they were still nine and ten."

Shea smiled. "Yeah, but you can tell they'd stop a bullet for each other."

"You're right about that." He glanced over at her. "They'll expect us for dinner. If you don't want to, say the word."

Her stomach lurched. "Oh, God."

"How about we stop at Marge's diner in town? I'll call Rachel. They'll understand."

She was tempted. But that meant reverting to the old Shea. She'd made too much progress moving forward to chicken out now. Anyway, she kind of owed the McAllisters. Dragging Jesse away wouldn't be nice. "No, we'll eat at the Sundance. If I'm invited, I accept."

"You're invited," he said with a short laugh. "I need you for protection."

"Me?"

"If my sister gets me alone she'll drive me nuts with the questions."

"About last night?"

"About you, mostly." He sent Shea an apologetic look. "I shouldn't have put my arm around you this morning. I tried for a poker face until I saw how scared you looked." He brought her hand to his lips and kissed the backs of her fingers. It gave her goose bumps. "I'm not going to lie to you. They're probably bursting with curiosity, but no one will say anything to you."

She bit back a smile. "Not even Rachel?"

Jesse looked as though he had to think about that one, and then groaned. "I'll take care of her as soon as we get home."

"No, don't say anything. I can handle it, really. And this morning…I wasn't scared, just overwhelmed." She plucked a small piece of hay that was stuck to his hair. "They were very kind and I was touched by their concern." She angled herself so that she rested her cheek on the seat and could watch him. He was clean-shaven now and she liked that look, too. "I can't believe we've only known each other a few days."

"I know." He glanced over at her. "Keep looking at me like that and I'm going to pull over and make love to you."

Shea grinned. "I'd let you."

He chuckled. "We're eating dinner fast, got that?"

Her toes curled. "Wow, a real bed and a warm room."

"Yep. And a whole box of condoms."

THE NEXT DAY Jesse waited until Shea left for Safe Haven in her rental. The roads were clear and no snow was coming down within a hundred-mile radius of Blackfoot Falls, so he didn't feel the need to go caveman on her and insist she not drive. If the weather changed, they agreed she'd stay put 'til he picked her up. He hated that tonight was the open house. It was going to be a zoo around here and he was running out of time.

He found Rachel in the den. "You got a minute?"

She looked up from her laptop. "Sure."

"I want to get Shea a gift." He glanced over his shoulder, not keen on anyone overhearing. "Any suggestions?"

"You know tomorrow is Christmas Eve already."

"Yep." He shrugged. "I have to go check on the Cessna

later, see if I can get her up soon. Then I figured I'd drive over to Kalispell and pick up something."

Frowning, she set the laptop aside and swung her stocking feet off the coffee table. "Honestly, I don't know her well enough to make a suggestion. You weren't thinking of jewelry, were you?"

He caught the teasing glint in her eye. "You think one carat is too chintzy?"

She blinked, and narrowed her gaze. "You lie."

"Yep, I lie. So are you gonna help me or not?"

Rachel grinned. "I might have a suggestion, which you probably won't like, and I could be way off base, but she doesn't strike me as being the materialistic type."

"Definitely not." He hated that he had to rely on Rachel for this, but he was notoriously bad at choosing gifts. "So?"

"We'll get to that. I want to say something while I have you here."

"Oh, God…"

"Shut up and listen. It's not horrible." She got up and walked over to him. "It's nice to see glimpses of the old Jesse," she said and gently hugged him. "That's all." When she leaned back, her eyes were moist.

He had to look away. "I know, Rach," he said quietly. What else could he say…? *By the way, I'm probably going to reenlist so don't get used to it?* The thought depressed him. Every part of it—having to tell the family, leaving Montana, putting on a uniform every day. And Shea? No, she wasn't a part of the equation. She'd be returning to California in a few days. "So what do you think for Shea?"

"Oats and corn," Rachel said with a decisive nod, then grinned at him. "Wish I had a camera. Think about it for a second. Remember how excited she was about taking the horses their 'treats'? Buy a few bags and tie a big red bow around them. You know how city people are about pets. Bet she'd love it."

After the initial absurdity of the suggestion passed, Jesse smiled. His sister was on to something. And he reckoned he knew an even better surprise.

He grabbed Rachel by the waist, ignoring her squeal of surprise when he lifted her off the floor and spun her around. "You rock, kiddo." He set her down. "I'll be out for a while."

"Don't forget you promised to help set up for tonight."

He stopped at the door. The open house. Damn.

"Go." Rachel made a shooing motion. "I'll get Trace to pitch in."

"Thank you," he said, feeling a stab of guilt when he met her hopeful green eyes. Then he took off before he said something stupid.

"Do you have any idea how long you've been staring at that tree?" Jesse touched the small of Shea's back and passed her the hot apple cider he'd gone to get for her from the spread in the dining room.

She smiled at him and folded her palms around the warm glass mug. "It's so beautiful I can't help it."

"Not the word I would've used to describe this one. The spruce in the living room, yeah." He squinted at the plaster gingerbread man. "That thing's got to be over twenty years old. Can't remember whose handiwork it is. Probably Cole's or mine."

"Cole. I saw his name on the back. That's yours." She pointed to the one with a misshapen foot.

Jesse grunted. "Figures mine is the messed-up one."

She frowned at him. "Stop it. He's adorable."

He just laughed and shrugged, but it bothered her that he'd said that.

She scanned the collection of homemade ceramic candy

canes, various Barbie doll accessories, the Disney character ornaments, the twinkling multicolored lights. "I want a tree like this someday. It kind of tells a story."

He slipped an arm around her, kissed the side of her neck and whispered, "I figured you liked it back here in the den because it's more private."

His lips tickled, and she giggled. "I haven't done too badly. I've socialized a bit. I met Sadie, who owns the Watering Hole, and Louise from the sewing shop."

"That's not what I meant." He nipped at her lower lip.

"Hey, I'll spill my cider." Two things had amazed her since people had begun showing up for the open house. She hadn't hidden in her room but actually had a few conversations. And then there was Jesse himself, who constantly surprised her with his unself-conscious displays of affection.

Nothing extreme or that made her uncomfortable. But he didn't shy away from holding her hand or sliding an arm around her shoulders in front of his family and neighbors.

"We've made our appearance," he said, obviously not caring if she spilled because now he had two arms around her. "Time to duck out."

"The stairs are in full view." She shook her head, aghast at the notion of anyone seeing them. "I'm not doing that."

"You have a point. Okay, I have another idea." He drew back and took her hand.

"Where are we going?"

Without answering he led her out of the den and through the living room, past the ten-foot tree decked out in white lights, white satin bows and white doves. An elderly couple chatted with Barbara by the grandfather clock. Several kids were inspecting the hand-stitched stockings hanging above the huge stone fireplace. The whole room smelled of pine from the trees and the yards and yards of fresh garland strung across the mantel and up the staircase railings.

The house seemed made for entertaining. Each large room spilled into the next, and people dressed in jeans and festive shirts were everywhere—lingering at the buffet table in the open dining room, gathering around the wet bar opposite the fireplace or crowding the kitchen and foyer.

"Whoo-hoo…look who's got himself a girl." A brunette carrying a toddler on her hip came from the kitchen grinning at Jesse. "Congratulations, honey," she said to Shea as she passed. "This one's always been too slippery to catch."

"Evening, Doreen," he said dryly, shaking his head.

Shea playfully elbowed him. "Who is she?"

"My eighth-grade girlfriend."

"I bet you had a lot of them."

"I wouldn't say a *lot*."

"Don't let him kid you." Rachel surprised them from behind. "All the girls went cross-eyed over my quiet, mysterious brother. Where are you guys off to?"

"None of your business, squirt."

"Don't get stranded anywhere, huh?" With a cheeky grin Rachel veered off toward the table set up with punch and eggnog.

They'd almost made it to the front door when a young couple Jesse had gone to school with intercepted them. Jesse was polite, introduced her, asked about their kids, then excused himself, promising he'd get together with them in the new year.

"Finally," he said, when they stepped outside.

He'd spoken too soon. The smokers had gathered in the chilly night air and lined the wraparound porch. Shea let Jesse do the talking, impressed at how smoothly and quickly he extricated them from the group.

She was breathless by the time they entered the dimly lit barn. "What are we doing here?" she asked, glancing around at the equipment and odd shapes made stranger by the shadows. The building was clearly big, but on the inside it seemed as if it went on forever.

"Looking for privacy." He tugged at her hand and she went into his arms for a kiss that was too brief. "Wait right here."

She did as he asked, rubbing her arms and wishing she wore more than a lightweight red sweater. She didn't even have thermals under her jeans. But, of course, she hadn't planned on leaving the house. For that matter, she hadn't intended to stay at the party for more than a few minutes and had only gone to be polite. Except Jesse made everything easier. His whole family did, really, and each day it felt more natural to listen with interest and participate in conversations even if she hadn't initiated them herself.

The creaking sound of a door had her peering intently into a dark corner of the barn. Jesse had headed that way. That didn't mean they were alone. "Jesse?" she called quietly.

"It's me. I keep meaning to oil the hinges." He walked into the muted glow provided by the intermittent security lights with something draped over his arm.

"What is that?"

"A blanket." His teeth flashed white.

She laughed. "You're not serious."

"Dare you to find out." He took her hand again and pulled her toward the ladder to the hayloft.

"Is this where you brought all your girlfriends?"

"Okay…look, I only had two in high school and one in college. Happy?" He tapped her backside and motioned for her to go first up the rungs.

"What about grade school?"

"Doesn't count."

"Then what about—"

Jesse's mouth covered hers, cutting her off. He took advantage of her parted lips, pushing his tongue inside, hot and demanding, until she struggled for air.

As he drew back he touched her tightened nipple through her sweater. "You want to get up there before somebody catches us."

"There better not be any strange animals up there," she said, grabbing hold of the rails and putting a foot on the first rung.

"Oh, yeah, there might be a cat, so don't scream. Luther's harmless."

She felt Jesse come up behind her, but he didn't crowd her as she took her time to find her footing.

The loft wasn't as pitch-black as she'd expected. Ambient light from below helped guide her to a spot where she waited for him to catch up.

"There's a small floodlight up here," he said while shaking out the blanket. "But I don't want to draw attention."

"I'm sensing a trend here—you like roughing it, don't you?"

"If it was up to me we'd be in my room getting naked." Hooking an arm around her waist, he hauled her against him. "But I'll settle for making out." He traced her ear with the tip of his tongue. "Unless you'd rather go back to the party."

A teasing remark about the dirt she could get on him never made it past her brain. She sighed at the feel of his lips grazing the side of her neck, and when he started using his teeth to gently scrape right where he knew it drove her crazy, she sank to the blanket, pulling him down with her.

The floor underneath wasn't nearly as hard as she'd expected. But of course Jesse suffered the brunt of it by cradling her to him. He pulled her the rest of the way onto his lap while he kept kissing her, and she couldn't understand why his kisses seemed different each time. Even when all they had time for was a brief brushing of lips it seemed more passionate. The thought that soon there would be no more kisses nearly crippled her. She turned her mind to more pleasant thoughts.

"Are you comfortable?" he asked.

"Very." She loved being right here, her cheek pressed to Jesse's heart. "The first time I saw you was in this barn."

He shifted to look at her. "When?"

"The day I arrived. You were standing at the door. I thought you were one of the hired hands."

"Most people claim they can spot a McAllister from a mile away."

"I can see that…eventually I would've noticed the resemblance, but that day Cole and Jamie drove in behind me. Your mom, Rachel and Trace all came out to greet them but you watched from the shadows."

"I was probably too grubby."

For the first time, Jesse had lied to her. She didn't know what gave her that impression. Maybe it was his slight hesitation or the increase of his heartbeat but she was fairly sure she wasn't wrong. "You seem to like Jamie so I've wondered about that."

"Jamie's great. She's perfect for Cole. The whole family's crazy about her."

"Think they'll get married?"

"Hmm. I hadn't thought about it. They've only known each other five months, but I wouldn't be surprised."

Shea pulled back to look at him. "You're kidding."

"She was a guest here the second week Rachel opened."

"I assumed they'd known each other for years." Shea thought back to the few times she'd been around them. They were so comfortable together. The entire family treated Jamie as if they'd known her forever.

"You're quiet." He slid his hand under her sweater.

"Huh? Oh, I was just thinking about how everyone seems to love Jamie. It's nice." She was a little jealous, but she wouldn't admit that part. "Jamie's an easy person to like."

"So are you." He unfastened her bra clasp.

"You don't have to say that. It's not true. I know I don't let people in. It's not in my nature."

"No, it's not, and there's nothing wrong with being introverted. Some people would say the same about me."

"You?" Shea smiled. "You know everyone."

"I've lived here most of my life. Of course I know everybody, and sometimes I wish I didn't."

That surprised her. But then it wasn't so easy to think now that he'd pushed aside her bra and palmed her breast. "But you came back. You love it here."

There was another one of those tense pauses. "I do, but… Jesus." He withdrew his hand.

She moved off his lap.

"What are you doing?" He sounded irritated.

"Trying not to ruin our night."

"Nobody's going to ruin anything."

She held his face in her hands and kissed him. "You can tell me anything, or you can tell me nothing. We introverts have to stick together."

He flashed a smile. "I wish we were in my room right now."

"Me, too."

The words were barely out of her mouth when she heard something. Voices. Just outside. Jesse heard them, too, because he tensed and put a finger to her lips.

She nodded.

The voices grew louder and closer.

"Kids," he whispered. "Probably in here sneaking a beer. We'll wait them out."

She nodded again.

Then Jesse pulled up her sweater, rubbed her nipple between his thumb and forefinger and she slapped a hand across her own mouth to keep from crying out.

16

JESSE KNEW SHE couldn't make a sound, and he was relentless. His mouth, his hands…they were everywhere. The rat was enjoying holding her hostage. She'd think of a way to pay him back, she decided. But for now she pressed her lips together, closed her eyes and shivered when he slowly unzipped her jeans.

Below them the kids—sounded like two boys and a girl—were talking and laughing and giving no indication they were in a hurry to leave the barn. Luckily they'd moved deeper into the building and weren't directly beneath the loft, but still…

Shea sucked in a breath, but that only made it easier for him to slide his hand inside her panties. With his other hand he pushed up the hem of her sweater and bared her breasts. Since it was too dark to see, he found his way with his mouth. He latched on to her nipple and drove her crazy with quick featherlike flicks of his tongue.

His hair was short but she managed to grab two handfuls. She tried to force him to stop, which he finally did, in his own good time, and only so that he could kiss her until she was breathless. She let him lay her back, slowly, quietly, and when she was able to reach, she stroked the heel of her palm up his fly.

Even through the thick denim his erection felt hot and urgent. He was turned on. For her. She thought about that comment about Jesse being too slippery to catch. But here he was, with Shea, wanting her. Wanting her so badly that he couldn't wait until they were able to sneak upstairs. And that was after having made love twice this morning. The hugeness of the idea was almost too much to hold inside her head.

She found the tab of his zipper, but he was too hard for her to pull it down easily. He must've realized she wasn't giving up and he took over the job. Greedily, she reached inside his jeans and closed her hand around his erection. He hissed through clenched teeth and jerked against her palm. A nervous giggle tickled the back of her throat and she shuddered trying to quash it.

Jesse leaned in, his lips close to her ear, and whispered, "Do something for me."

She nodded.

"Lie back. Let me touch you."

His request confused her. He hadn't stopped touching her. Then he moved her hand away from his cock, placing it palm down on the floor beside her hip, and she understood. It was going to be torture not moving, not uttering a sound, not touching him back. Incredibly sexy, too.

Vaguely she was aware that the kids were still below, their voices no more than indistinct murmurs. She'd have to watch herself and not get carried away. Not easy when Jesse was teasing and licking his way from her collarbone to her neck. One of his hands threaded through her hair, lightly massaging her scalp. The other worked the waistband of her jeans, inching it lower until he embedded his fingers beneath the denim.

She fisted her hands and pressed her lips together as he dragged his mouth over her breasts and then lower.

His jaw was smooth on her belly. He'd shaved recently, probably right before the party. His beard grew quickly and it was dark and dense. And when he was careful not to mark her, God, how she loved the feel of his chin's rasp on her skin first thing in the morning. But then she also liked the silky feel of it at the end of the day when they crawled into bed.

Since being stranded in the shack, they'd also spent a night together in her room. They'd agreed hers was the best option. Located in the guest wing, it was safely away from the family. She could swear his new mission in life was to make her scream. He shoved her jeans and panties past her knees, and she bit her lip hard to avoid gasping. Cool hands spread her thighs as far as they could go, then his hot tongue parted her. She rolled her head, tried to grab Jesse, but as he zeroed in on her swollen clitoris, she had to use the heel of her hand to silence her cries.

Good God, he was going to drive her out of her mind between the flicking and the sucking. This time Shea did get hold of Jesse's hair, and she tugged twice, wishing she could shout at him to stop so they could go somewhere private—though the threat of getting caught made her tremble even harder.

"Give me one of those." A male voice that hadn't lowered in pitch yet broke the silence.

The kids had moved. It sounded as though they'd relocated directly below the loft.

"You guys know better than to smoke in here," the girl said, and Shea felt Jesse tense and go still.

"Relax. I'll be careful."

"You light that cigarette and I'm going back to the house. I mean it."

Someone struck a match.

"Fine. See you guys later," the girl said, and Jesse moved his hand and sat up.

"Damn. Wait. Okay. I'm putting it out."

"It's too cold out here, anyway." The girl's voice had already faded as though she'd left the barn.

Jesse sighed and pushed Shea's pants up her thighs. She took over while he moved up and ran the back of his hand gently across her cheek. "I bet they light up again," he whispered in her ear, then brought her sweater down.

He got to his feet, and she sat up, fumbling to fasten her bra. Sure enough, the striking of a match echoed in the silence. Jesse snapped and zipped his jeans while she took care of hers. Then he motioned for her to stay put.

He didn't head for the ladder but moved to the edge of the loft. "You boys had better not be smoking," he said in a low, stern voice.

"Shit!"

The kid's high-pitched squeak made Shea bite her lip to keep from laughing.

"We're leaving." The other boy had a deeper timbre.

"Good idea." Jesse stood with his arms crossed, watching, presumably until the boys left the barn.

"Could they see you?" she asked when he turned back to her. "Did they know it was you?"

"They wouldn't look up. I know their parents but not them personally."

"Poor guys."

"Yeah, right. They're ranch kids. They damn well know better than to be smoking around this much hay."

"Plus, they ruined the mood."

Jesse chuckled. "My mood is just fine." Taking her hand, he pulled her to her feet and put his arms around her.

She looped hers around his neck and moved her hips against him. He wasn't as hard as before, but getting there. Evidently he was right. The interruption had been nothing but a speed bump for him. "What do we do now?"

"What do you think?"

Shea laughed. "Someone else could show up."

"We're going inside."

"We still have the same problem whether we go to your room or mine. Both sets of stairs are in full view."

He kissed her lips softly, tenderly. "You go up first. I'll follow ten minutes later." He lightly rubbed her nose with his. Hugging her tighter, he heaved a slow contented sigh that tugged at her heart. "On our way out I'll turn on more lights."

"Think they'll come back?"

"Not them, but others might have the same idea. Ready?"

She nodded and stood back to dust off her clothes. "Remind me never to wear this sweater for a roll in the hay again. It's like a magnet."

Jesse laughed. "Roll in the hay?"

"Yes, I'm getting the cowboy lingo down."

"I've never used that term in my life." He plucked hay off her left breast, then cupped its weight. "Of course, I'm not much of a cowboy," he murmured.

"You're not helping." It was crazy how easily he could have talked her into sinking back down to the blanket. She had no willpower when it came to him. Scary. Except it wasn't. Jesse seemed more familiar to her than Brian ever had, even after they'd lived together nearly three years.

His odd remark finally clicked. "What do you mean you're not much of a cowboy?" In answer, he kneaded her breast, and she swatted his hand away. She bent and scooped up the blanket before either of them got any stupid ideas. "Why did you say that?"

"I don't know." His sigh was far from contented now. He sounded annoyed. "The blanket's full of hay. It's getting all over you."

All right, she wouldn't press. But she hated the feeling his words and grim tone had left her with. The blanket was already folded in half, and she folded it in half again. He was right…more hay had stuck to her sweater. "Well, this is great. No guessing where we've been and what we were doing."

"Leave it." He took the blanket from her and tossed it onto a railing. "I'll take care of it tomorrow."

"Okay." She smiled, even though her face was in shadow and he couldn't see her. Continuing to dust herself off, she headed toward the ladder.

"Wait." Jesse exhaled sharply. "That was a thoughtless remark. It doesn't mean anything."

"Fine. I won't give the matter a second thought." She touched his face to reassure him, and he caught her hand.

He gave it a gentle squeeze. "Cole and Trace, they've been here through the hard times. After our dad died, Cole poured his heart and soul into learning every aspect of running this place. His entire life has been dedicated to this ranch. Even Trace, for all his strutting and horsing around, worked his ass off while his high school friends spent their weekends partying. Trace never complained. The Sundance always came first. He's a smart guy and could've done well in college but he didn't go. Didn't even give it a try. He chose to stay here and help Cole."

"College isn't for everyone," she said calmly, trying to ease his mounting tension. God, why now, why here? She'd suspected something was eating at Jesse and she very much wanted to hear him out. But they needed privacy, a place to sit without fear of someone disturbing them. She could suggest they continue in her room, though she had the feeling that once he stopped talking, he'd withdraw again. He'd shut her out. "Do you regret choosing a different path than your brothers?"

"Not really. Cole went for a year of school before Dad was diagnosed but he hated being cooped up in a classroom. He quit and came home. Even when the place was making money, he and Trace were outside working right alongside the hands.

They love the land. They love what they do. There's nothing else for them but the Sundance. The ranch is their life."

"And that's a bad thing?" There was no place to sit except for a bale of hay. She looped an arm through his and steered him toward it.

"Where are we going?"

"Right here." She sat first and hoped he'd follow suit.

He hesitated, and she held her breath, hoping the moment hadn't been lost. Finally he lowered himself to the spot next to her, letting his thigh touch hers.

Shea shifted so that their upper arms touched, too. Oh, how she wished she was better at this. Did Jesse need the closeness, or would she scare him off? Should she simply listen, reserve comment? She had no idea what he expected from her, or how she could best be his friend.

One thing she knew for sure, she didn't want to be this frustrated and nervous while they talked. She breathed in deeply, slowly let it out, repeated the exercise, letting go of anything that might interfere with the moment.

"We should go inside." He shifted, moving his leg slightly away from hers.

She clasped her hands together, sick that she'd already failed. "Talk to me," she said.

"There's not much to say. I don't know why I brought up that crap." He sighed.

"Must be a reason." Her voice shook a little. She hoped he hadn't noticed. But she couldn't worry about it. All her energy was focused on staying put and not running away because this was hard. Outside her comfort zone by a mile. But this was also Jesse. She had to see this conversation through.

He'd turned to look at her. The light was better here near the wall, and he could see her face. She could see part of his, though not his eyes. "What's wrong?" he asked, closing one large hand over both of hers.

"Please don't try to change the subject or make this about me. I want to hear about you."

He frowned. "I'm not doing anything. You're shaking."

"Oh." Her tiny whimper of defeat sounded pathetic. No, she wouldn't crumble. Not now. "Look, I want to be here for you, be your sounding board, but I'm really bad at this kind of thing and all I want to do... God, Jesse, I don't want to screw up...." She stared down at their entwined hands. "Will you just talk to me?"

Even though she'd averted her gaze, she felt his stare. She'd said too much. Why couldn't she have kept her mouth shut? She should've bolted while she could. It was so much safer.

He let go of her hands, and her heart sank. Then he slid his arm around her and pulled her against him. His body was warm and his heartbeat steady. He kissed her hair, gently rubbed her arm. She felt safe. The idea was startling and intimate, and ironically reignited the urge to run. But she understood a lifelong habit couldn't be overcome in one night.

Still shell-shocked, she almost laughed. A few minutes ago she'd been trying to calm herself in order to soothe him. Now he was doing it for her.

"You're brave," he whispered.

"I'm not. I'm really not."

He smiled against her cheek, then kissed her. "Remember the other day at the shack when I told you about how I offered to quit school after my dad passed away?" he asked, and Shea nodded. "When my mom and Cole told me it wasn't necessary, that I should finish college, I was mad. I thought they were being stubborn and irrational, but more than that—" he took a deep breath "—I felt useless. Disposable. They might as well have said they didn't need me."

"Oh, Jesse..." She twisted around to look at him. "That isn't true. They would never feel that way. Not your family."

She stared into his shadowed eyes, hoping she could make him see. "Never."

"Yeah, you're right." He shrugged, and she wasn't sure he believed his own words. "I was young and grieving and trying to find my way in life. I really wanted to come home, share the burden and make this ranch the best spread in the county. Like any kid, I wanted my parents to be proud of me. Even though my dad was gone, I imagined him smiling down at me, thinking that's my son, a true McAllister. He belongs at the Sundance."

"Your mom does feel that way—your brothers, Rachel, they all do."

He gave her a faint smile and squeezed her thigh. "You just met them."

"I don't care." She shook her head. "I know I'm usually not a good judge of people, but I'm not wrong about this. The morning Cole and Trace brought us home, when I was sitting in the kitchen with your mom and Rachel… They were being so nice. They were genuinely concerned for me, and I was feeling weird, not knowing how to act or what to say, and then I had this epiphany." She'd spoken so fast she had to stop to take a breath. "All my life my value has been my intelligence. I wasn't appreciated for being kind or funny or for simply being a child. I was my father's pet, my mother's pawn, my teachers' greatest accomplishment.

"As I got older nothing changed. My classmates, coworkers, Brian, my boss, everyone around me reinforced what I'd learned as a kid. I was expected to produce. Social participation, not necessary. My IQ defined me and everyone I've ever known has wanted something from me. Except you, Jesse. And your family. You don't care how smart I am or if I'm going to make stockholders rich. I sat in your kitchen and realized that the McAllisters just want to be sure I'm okay." She swallowed a lump of emotion. "So you see, even clueless, inept me knows something about your family. Don't underestimate them. You do them a disservice."

She'd gone too far. Said too much. He was staring at her with the same remote expression he'd worn that morning in the kitchen. She could barely see any sign of the Jesse she knew. Damn him. Damn herself for sticking her nose into matters about which she knew nothing.

Still, she didn't shut up. "You're not useless, not then, not now," she said with a fierceness she hadn't known she possessed. "I bought in to everyone's crap and stayed nice and safe inside my bubble. I threw myself into my work. So I admit, feeling as if I don't belong is partly on me. I let it happen. Because now if I'm not the best at what I do, I'm worse than useless, I'm nothing. Your family loves you. You matter. That's not a small thing."

She felt drained. Stunned that she'd revealed so much about herself. But she had to get up, be sure she could stand. Make it down the ladder and then to her room.

She almost made it to her feet when he pulled her onto his lap. "Don't go," he whispered, his voice husky.

She buried her face in his shoulder. Her eyes were moist and he didn't need to see that. If she'd gotten through to him, it was worth having exposed herself.

"You must think I'm a selfish, thoughtless bastard," he murmured, his breath warm on her neck.

"Of course I don't."

"You're really something, Shea Monroe," he said, leaning back so he could tip her chin up and look her in the eyes. "Thank you."

Shea inhaled a shaky breath, which was a good thing because a moment later he stole it away with a kiss.

AT THE BACK DOOR, Shea had decided she wanted to stick to the plan of separately sneaking up to her room. But that meant anyone loitering in the kitchen had a view of the stairs leading up to the guest wing. Luckily only two women were gabbing at the table. Jesse distracted them while Shea slipped upstairs. She owed him big for having to endure Mrs. Wilcox's drawn-out recounting of her latest bout with shingles.

He knocked twice at Shea's door before letting himself in. She lay stretched out on the queen-size bed, naked, the cream-colored sheets draped over her hips. Her pretty pink nipples were already puckered and beckoning him, yet all he could do was stand there and stare, his heart slamming his chest.

Her debt for the Wilcox ordeal? Paid in full.

She smiled, then blew at the long bangs getting in her eyes. "What kept you?"

He'd already jerked the buttons free, and he shrugged out of his shirt, dropping it on the wood floor as he walked toward her.

His boots and jeans came off next. But he made sure he grabbed the condom out of his pocket before he chucked the Levi's. God, he wanted her with a desperation that wasn't like him. But then Shea stirred all kinds of unfamiliar feelings. He'd told her things…things he'd never said aloud.

How could someone so sweet and inexperienced reduce him to mindless mush? He hadn't been thinking about his future, about the epic decision he had to make. The truth was, reenlisting was looking like a less viable option. When he was with her, or even thinking about being with her, life seemed perfect. She thought she was different, clueless. She was so wrong. Shea Monroe was wiser and more in touch with reality than anyone he knew.

And brave. So damn brave. Sharing her innermost fears and hurdles with him to help him see that he might have made some wrong assumptions, himself. She'd given him a lot to think about. But right now he had to have her.

She looked absolutely beautiful lying there, her hair spread out, color high in her cheeks as she waited… For him.

"What's wrong?" she asked softly, worrying her lower lip, her gray-blue eyes growing dark with concern, probably because he'd been motionless, staring.

"Nothing," he said, pulling back the sheet and crawling in beside her. "Just thinking how beautiful you look."

Her lips parted in protest. He covered them with an open-mouthed kiss, using his tongue with a thoroughness he hoped expressed something for which he couldn't find the words.

He moved down to kiss each breast, her stomach, each hip bone while he sheathed himself.

She spread her thighs for him, and he positioned himself between them, using all his willpower not to just bury himself inside her. He leaned over, framed her face with his hands and looked into her eyes as he slowly entered her until they were as close as two people could be. Then she lifted her hips and clutched his shoulders. That was all he could stand.

He began to move, and she was right there, so in sync it was as if they'd done this a thousand times before, that their bodies had a language of their own. Neither of them looked away, they barely blinked. The connection was as real as the heat between her legs, as the rush that started in the deepest part of him until he couldn't hold back.

A low moan of pleasure tore from her throat as she trembled with her own release. And damn if he didn't hold on to her as if he never wanted to let go.

17

CHRISTMAS MORNING DAWNED bright and sunny, the air inside the house fragrant with pine, sweet rolls and coffee as Shea descended the stairs, trying to shake her worry over the still-missing Caleb. Everyone was on the lookout for the roan, and there wasn't anything more she could do, so she needed to focus on the moment. On Christmas.

Jesse had left earlier to feed and water the stabled horses while she'd showered, and it surprised her that she wasn't the least bit nervous to enter the kitchen alone. Even knowing she'd have to make small talk with Barbara, Rachel and anyone else who was responsible for the heavenly smells making her tummy growl. Mostly, though, she was excited. So very happy.

Yesterday, after her shift at Safe Haven and Jesse's return from delivering the Cessna to the airstrip, the whole family sat down to dinner. They'd automatically included her in their tradition of giving each other small wrapped gag gifts, hers and Jamie's contributions thoughtfully provided by Rachel, and singing carols in front of the fire.

The three guys refused to sing, apparently also an annual custom, but that didn't stop them from laughing at Rachel's and Jamie's off-key renditions of the holiday favorites. Shea escaped ridicule by lip-syncing. Trace had called her on it, and instead of being embarrassed, she'd felt included. Last night had been the best Christmas Eve ever.

"Merry Christmas!" Rachel and Jamie said at the same time when they saw her come through the door. They were sitting at the table with steaming mugs, sharing a cinnamon bun.

Unexpectedly emotional, Shea opened her mouth to respond in kind and found her voice wouldn't work. She just stared at them for a second and then said, "Oh." She cleared her throat and lied. "I haven't used my voice yet."

Rachel cracked up, then with a sly wink, said, "Yeah, guess my brother isn't much of a talker this early."

Jamie rolled her eyes. "God, Rachel, we really need to get you hooked up. I promise they had better things to do than talk."

Shea's cheeks got a bit warm. Of course *everyone* knew about her and Jesse sleeping together but no one had said anything.

Rachel groaned. "No kidding. This dry spell is killing me. Good ol' Blackfoot Falls," she muttered. "Screw it." She stood. "I want my own disgustingly fattening bun."

Jamie thought that was pretty funny. Smiling, Shea crossed to the coffeepot, again struck by the impossible idea that Jamie had only known everyone for a few months.

"Rachel, get back to the table. You, too, Shea." Jamie glanced over her shoulder at the door, then waited for them to join her. "Cole and I planned to tell everyone later, but I can't wait. And he laughed at my singing last night so the hell with it. But I'm only telling the two of you so don't say anything."

Jamie sat across from them, excitement dancing in her face, as she cast a last glance toward the door.

"All right, already," Rachel said. "Jeez, tell us."

Mirroring Rachel, Shea leaned closer. Her heart leaped

and her breath quickened. They'd never understand the poignancy of this moment for her. Especially with Jamie looking from Rachel to Shea and back again. Shea belonged to this little group, right here, right now. She totally belonged.

"I'm moving here," Jamie said, her hazel eyes shining. "Right after the holidays. I'm packing up everything, selling my condo and then I'll start working from—"

"Oh, my God." Rachel jumped up. Her chair flew backward. She rounded the table, her arms open. "Oh, my God. Jamie. This is so awesome." They hugged for a long moment, then Rachel moved back, dabbing at her eyes.

"Congratulations," was all Shea could think to say.

"Thanks." Jamie beamed. "I travel a lot, and that won't change much for now, but in between I basically work from home. As long as I have my computer, I'm good."

"I can't believe it." Rachel sniffed. "Cole and I will be fighting over you," she said, and they all laughed. Then Rachel looked at Shea. "You work with a computer, don't you? God, if you moved here, too, that would be so cool."

Shea let out a short laugh, startled. Her heart had begun pounding, but really, what could she say to something so crazy?

"Okay..." Cole's amused drawl broke up the party. He walked into the kitchen, shaking his head. "I'm betting someone couldn't keep her mouth shut," he said as he pulled Jamie into his arms.

She tilted her head back, and with a haughty smile said, "You've never complained about my mouth before."

A grin tugging at his lips, Cole kissed her.

"Gross," Rachel said in a whiny twelve-year-old voice. She carried her mug to the counter, grinning at Shea.

At the sudden pressure on the small of her back, Shea started. It was Jesse, who'd apparently come in directly behind Cole. His dark fathomless eyes met hers, and she held her breath wondering what he'd heard. She hoped he didn't think there had been any instigation on her part. Anyway, Rachel had been joking.

His gaze only wavered when he slid a possessive arm around her shoulders and whispered, "I think it would be very cool."

HOURS LATER, snuggled up next to Jesse in his truck, Shea yawned, tired from a full day and it was only late afternoon. They turned down the driveway to the Sundance followed by Jamie, Cole, Trace and Rachel riding in Cole's huge black pickup.

Christmas breakfast had not been the leisurely affair she'd expected. She'd known straight off she had time for only a cameo because she'd refused to leave Annie alone to handle the day's chores. What had stunned Shea was the announcement Trace made when she'd tried to excuse herself from the table. The whole family was going to Safe Haven to help. Everyone except Barbara, who stayed behind to get a jump on dinner preparations.

Jesse glanced over at her. "Don't fall asleep. We still have dinner and presents."

She winced. "I didn't buy you anything, Jesse. It was such a crazy week."

He picked up her hand and kissed the back. "I have what I want."

Her heart fluttered. Since this morning it had been hard to shut out what he'd said in the kitchen. Or to not think about Jamie's upcoming move. Her job as a travel blogger allowed her to live anywhere. Shea wasn't in quite the same situation, but the fact remained that a computer was all Shea needed, as well.

A week ago, the mere idea of leaving her job would have seemed preposterous. God, hadn't she suffered enough change in the past year? But several times today when she'd been seeing to the sick horses or feeding and playing with the goats, she'd fantasized about what it would be like to work permanently at a place like Safe Haven. She'd never thought of herself as an outdoor person…for good reason. She wasn't, not even a little. But thinking about being stuck at a desk for fourteen hours a day really got to her.

And then there was Jesse. Of course he was part of the equation. Leaving him would be the hardest thing she'd ever done in her life. But her logical brain refused to give her feelings for him unrealistic weight. She'd learned too much about herself in the past year to backslide now.

What she had to do was stop thinking. Shame on her if she ruined her nearly perfect Christmas. Only two things would've made her day better—if Caleb had been found, and if Annie had accepted the McAllisters' dinner invitation.

Jesse parked in his normal spot and turned off the ignition, but he made no move to get out. He angled toward her and brushed aside her bangs. "What's going on? You don't look happy."

"I was thinking about Annie. I know she adores your family. She never goes anywhere unless she needs something for Safe Haven. I wish she'd given in and come to dinner."

"The holidays are a hard time for some people. Others prefer to be alone." His mouth curved faintly. "I get that. I don't know Annie well, but since she moved here she's been a loner."

"Yeah, I get the solitary part, too." Hard to believe after this past week.

He cupped the back of her neck and pulled her in for a long slow kiss.

Cole had parked somewhere behind them. Someone honked the pickup's horn.

From the back window, Jesse made a gesture with his hand

she couldn't see but it wasn't hard to guess. With a laugh, she broke the kiss.

"Children," he muttered irritably.

"And you were so mature."

Grinning, he opened his door. She heard her side open at the same time.

It was Trace. "Everyone helps Mom with dinner."

Jesse sighed. "Shea, elbow him for me, would you?"

She slid out of the truck and kissed Trace's cheek. "Thank you for helping today."

"Hey, no problem." He lifted his Stetson and resettled it, then headed for the house.

Chuckling, Jesse took her hand. "You caught the kid off guard. Doesn't happen often."

"Him? God, I can't believe I did that."

"Yet you survived. How about that?"

Sighing contentedly, she leaned into his side, and hands held tightly, they followed Trace. As soon as they made it through the front door, the craziness began.

Everybody pitched in to finish dinner, and within a couple of hours the meal was on the table and they'd all eaten their fill. Trace cleared the dishes without complaint, for which he received a standing ovation from Rachel and Jamie.

Next came the opening of presents. Shea had thought it was a bit strange to wait until the evening but she discovered the McAllisters didn't exchange gifts so there wasn't much to the ritual. Instead they chose two needy families in the county, provided them each with a side of beef for their freezer and lavished the children with wrapped toys and clothes.

Against Barbara's wishes, however, Rachel and the guys had bought her something. She'd gingerly opened the beautifully wrapped package, teared up as she smoothed her hand over the soft cashmere coat, then scolded her children for their extravagance.

The only other gifts under the tree were the ones Jamie had brought for each member of the family. Shea was touched but embarrassed that Jamie even had a present for her…a pretty hunter-green scarf Jamie had picked up in Kalispell after meeting Shea.

After the wrapping paper was collected and disposed of, Barbara left the group to make some phone calls. Cole and Jamie took their cue and disappeared, and Trace announced he was headed to a poker game in the bunkhouse with the two hands who'd elected not to go home for the holiday.

"Come with me to the barn," Jesse said, when Rachel excused herself, explaining she still had Christmas cards to open.

Shea stared at him in disbelief. "Seriously?"

"No, not that." He smiled. "I have something for you."

"Oh, no." Shea groaned. "Don't do this," she said, resisting when he rose and tried to pull her up with him.

"What's wrong? You'll like this…I promise."

"Don't you understand—"

"No." He forced her to her feet and led her to the back door, where their jackets hung on hooks in the mudroom.

Although he appeared calm, she sensed his excitement, and felt his quickening pulse as he practically dragged her toward the barn.

"I have nothing for you," she muttered, miserable.

"I told you." He squeezed her hand. "I have what I want."

His sweet gesture did little to pacify her. "But it's your fault," she said. "You monopolized all of my free time."

"You complaining?" Grinning, he flipped on the barn lights, stole a quick kiss, then motioned with his chin. "Merry Christmas, sweetheart," he said, slipping behind her and circling his arms around her waist.

She let him draw her back against his chest as she stared

at her gift. Bags of oats and corn were stacked four feet high and tied with a big sloppy red bow.

He rested his chin on her shoulder so that their cheeks touched, his arms tightening around her waist. "Am I forgiven?"

Shea laughed with complete delight. "I—I can't believe you did this. It's perfect." Emotion rose in her chest. "It's the nicest present I've ever—" She had to swallow. "Oh, Jesse…" Overwhelmed, she turned around in his arms and kissed his chin, then his cheek, though she'd been aiming for his mouth.

"Hold on. There's more." He easily found her lips, but kept the kiss brief, practically a peck. "Come on."

"No, you can't possibly do better than this."

"Trust me," he said, his chocolate-brown eyes melting her.

And because she did trust him, completely and unconditionally, she let him lead her out of the barn, past the corral while she struggled to deal with the avalanche of emotions clouding her ability to think. In less than a week her life had changed. *She'd* changed. And yet she couldn't see how that was possible. Even her parents had said she sounded different when she'd called them this morning. Not just her father, but her mother, who was normally oblivious to everything that didn't pertain to her.

But more incredible…what had nagged her most since this morning…she didn't miss work. Didn't miss the safe routine of going to her office, feeling secure in the knowledge that she was the best in her field and her computer never lied or judged.

So lost in thought, she hadn't realized they'd entered the stables until she heard one of the mares give a quiet nicker.

Shea blinked at Jesse. He stopped in front of the next stall. Didn't say a word, just waited, his gaze locked on her.

She frowned, wondering if he'd spoken and she hadn't

heard him. Then she turned her head to see if she could figure out what she'd missed.

Gasping, she clutched at her heart. She blinked rapidly at the beautiful strawberry-blond mane. Were her eyes playing a trick on her? "Caleb?" She stepped up to the stall, her outstretched hand trembling as she neared enough to touch him.

Ears pricked forward, he lowered his head and blew short and hard through his flared nostrils.

His warm breath hit her face, and her heart soared at his offer of friendship. "You remember me, don't you, sweetie?" she whispered. "I looked for you. I swear I didn't abandon you."

Jesse stroked her back. "I think he knows."

Emotion swelled in her throat and stung her eyes. She looked at him and saw that he was also affected. "How did you find him?"

"I got in touch with the guy who took him to Annie. He told me where he'd found Caleb. I figured it was worth a shot to check if he'd tried to make his way home." He shrugged. "I flew over the area, spotted him, called Trace and he brought a trailer."

"I can't believe this." God, she was going to cry.

As if reading her mind, in that wonderful low quiet voice of his, Jesse said, "You're allowed."

That pretty much pushed her over the edge and she buried her face against his shoulder. Still, she fought the tears, swallowing convulsively and squeezing her eyes shut. When Caleb neighed to get her attention, she pulled away from Jesse to stroke the roan's velvety muzzle.

"I don't want him to return to Safe Haven," she said, marveling at his beautiful coat. Someone had spent a lot of time grooming him…Jesse, of course. "I know Annie would take good care of him, but eventually she'd have to find him a home and I couldn't bear…"

"Caleb has a home. Don't you, boy?" Jesse rubbed the horse's mane, then looked at Shea. "He's staying here at the Sundance. He's yours. Whenever you want him, he'll be here."

She didn't trust her voice. She threw her arms around Jesse's neck. He staggered back, laughing. "I have to admit, deciding to find him was a tough call. I knew I'd probably lose out to the guy."

Laughing along with him, she hugged him tighter. "No, never. I love you both." It took her a few seconds to realize what she'd said, and she froze. Good God, what should she say or do now? Already the silent moment had stretched to awkwardness. "I, um…"

Jesse pried her arms from around his neck, and she forgot how to breathe. She'd scared him. He probably wanted to push her as far away as possible. How could she explain she didn't mean it? Not that way…except…God help her, what had she done? Had she fallen in love with him?

Sadly, it probably didn't matter, she thought as he drew away from her. She dropped her chin, finding it impossible to look at him.

He forced it up, wouldn't speak until she met his eyes.

"It's okay. I know how to share," he said with a crooked smile.

"Jesse…"

"Shh." He put a finger to her lips, then kissed her.

She kissed him back, hanging on to him for all she was worth. When they finally came up for air, she said, "Hey, it's still Christmas…." Grabbing his jacket, she backed up, tugging him along with her. "And I might have something for you, after all."

"Yeah?" Instantly getting her meaning, desire flared in his eyes. "Sorry, buddy," he said to Caleb as she pulled Jesse toward the door.

"I'll see you tomorrow, sweetie." She blew the roan an apologetic kiss.

"Huh, you call him sweetie."

Pleasure shimmered down her spine. She still wasn't sure this day was real. "What mushy name do you want me to call you?"

"Mushy?" Jesse smiled. "Surprise me."

They laughed like a pair of teenagers, then turned to race for the house. Their jackets were off by the time they made it to the mudroom, and hung seconds later. Trying to be quiet, they entered the kitchen and made it halfway to the guest stairs. That's when the bottom fell out.

"Jesse?" Cole's voice came from somewhere in the house.

Jesse hesitated. With a wry twist of his mouth, he looked at Shea and sighed. "Yeah."

Cole showed up at the door to the dining room. His expression seemed strained, his posture tense. "Would you come in here?"

"Now?"

His brother's frown deepened. "Now."

"What's up?" His back stiff, Jesse mirrored his brother's tension as he walked toward him.

In answer, Cole turned around and went back the way he'd come. Shea wasn't sure what to do. Something was very wrong. Jesse motioned for her to follow so she did.

Everyone but Trace was sitting in the living room. Shea was glad to see Jamie because her presence bolstered Shea's decision to stay. What made her wince was the grim set of Jamie's features. Rachel stood near the fireplace, appearing anxious and maybe a little angry. Barbara's eyes were red as though she'd been crying. A box of tissues sat beside her on the overstuffed couch.

When Cole turned around, no question he was angry.

His glare bore into Jesse as he passed him a piece of paper. "What's this?"

"Wait," Rachel said. "First of all, you need to know that I opened your mail by mistake. It was mixed in with the Christmas cards I picked up yesterday. That said, what the hell is the matter with you?"

Jesse gave no sign that he'd heard her. He continued to stare at the official-looking paper and wouldn't raise his eyes. The pulse at his neck beat double-time. His jaw had tightened.

"It's not what you think," he said finally. "I was just considering my options."

"But that you've even thought about it is insane," Rachel said, her green eyes glassy. "Look at Mom. She's a wreck." She went to sit with Barbara on the couch, but it was clear that whatever Jesse's alleged transgression, Rachel was also hurt.

Jesse exhaled sharply and moved to put a hand on his mother's shoulder. "Mom, I'm sorry."

"You didn't feel it was worth mentioning," Cole said in an even tone. "We're your family, Jesse. Reenlisting is one hell of an option considering what it would mean to the rest of us."

Shea jerked, feeling as if someone had slapped her. Jesse wanted to reenlist in the air force? Questions swirled through her mind so fast she literally felt dizzy. He'd never said, never hinted…

Barbara had captured Jesse's hand, pinning it to her shoulder. He didn't try to pull away, but looked over at Shea with stark eyes.

Rachel sniffed, then cleared her throat. "What do you think about his harebrained notion, Shea?"

She stood there, speechless, staring back at his family. Her knees were weak, her head light. For some reason her brain and mouth weren't connecting.

"She didn't know," Jesse said. "Leave her out of this."

Shea swallowed, having trouble even making her throat

work. How could she be hurt by his words? He was right. For a minute there she'd felt like a small part of the family, like she mattered to him. But in the end, nothing had changed in her tiny insular world.

"Excuse me," she murmured and turned around.

"Shea, wait."

She ignored Jesse, ignored everyone, yet managed to stay calm as she made it through the dining room to the kitchen. Once she was out of sight and earshot, she ran up the stairs to her room. She closed the door and leaned back against it for support.

Her heart raced. She pressed her palms to her cheeks. Her face was burning up. Why hadn't he told her? It wasn't as if she thought he'd been stringing her along for sex. Jesse wasn't like that. It was a matter of trust and sharing…and her being so hopelessly foolish. She'd let him in, bared her innermost fears and struggles. God, she'd told him everything. She'd thought he'd confided in her, as well. But he'd held back.

He had that right. She understood that at some level, but it still hurt that he hadn't considered her someone he could trust.

Letting her head fall back against the door, she closed her eyes. Maybe this was more about her than Jesse. How could she have fooled herself into believing she'd grown into a normal person in just a week? Clearly she was even more clueless than she'd imagined.

No. She refused to accept that. Coming to Montana had helped her. Jesse had helped her. So had working at Safe Haven. Because in spite of everything, she knew she no longer wanted her old life. She didn't want her only friend to be a computer.

Oh, God, she wanted Jesse.

Maybe his reenlisting was for the best. Not for his family, clearly, but for her. Shea adored Annie and what she was trying to accomplish, and Shea knew she could be an asset to the shelter. If she made the move, it didn't mean entirely giving up her job. Her boss needed her. They could work out something part-time.

So if Jesse reenlisted, she and everyone else would know her decision had nothing to do with him. Except that wasn't the complete truth. Pressing a hand to her queasy stomach, she slowly pushed away from the door.

If she didn't want to be sick, she had to get out of here.

JESSE STILL HAD some mending to do with his family. They were hurt and angry, and he didn't blame them. He'd been selfish, too caught up in his own bullshit to truly see their side or allow them a voice. But he did see the situation more clearly now, had for a couple days. Thanks to Shea.

He left them gathered in the living room with enough for them to rest easy for now. One thing they did get for sure… he had to talk to Shea. Make things right with her. Now.

His chest tight with fear and guilt, he climbed the stairs to her room. This wasn't going to be easy. He'd hurt her with his thoughtlessness, and he doubted his mind would ever be able to erase the look of devastation on her face as she'd fled. Part him of him expected her to refuse to talk to him, though that wasn't like Shea. But then who knew how much damage he'd done.

No matter what, he'd get her to listen, he thought, raising his fist to her door. No more being a coward. Too much was at stake. Jesus, he couldn't imagine her gone from his life.

She didn't answer his first knock or his second. He tried a third time. Was she ignoring him, or was she gone? His heart thudded. He turned the knob. It wasn't locked. He had no damn business opening her door uninvited. He did anyway.

The bed was still made. With relief he saw her suitcase sitting on the luggage rack. But there was no sign of her. She wouldn't be anywhere else in the house, but he had a damn good idea where she'd gone.

He hurried back down the stairs, saw her jacket still on the hook in the mudroom and didn't stop for his. It was freezing outside, about fifteen degrees. Walking briskly, his heart slamming his chest, he barely felt the chill wind, but it finally registered that he should've brought her jacket.

Only the stable's security lights were on, but he saw her standing in Caleb's open stall, her cheek pressed to his neck while she stroked the roan's side. She didn't see him. With an agitated whinny, Caleb alerted her to Jesse's presence. So the horse was mad at him, too.

Shea gave a start and looked over at him, then sharply turned away and dabbed at her eyes. He slowed his pace, giving her time. What he wanted to do was pull her into his arms and beg her forgiveness. That wouldn't be enough. He owed her so much more.

"You should be wearing your jacket," he said, stopping a safe distance out of reach and jamming his hands in his pockets.

"You, too." She kept her gaze on Caleb, repeatedly stroking his ribs with a trembling hand.

"I'm sorry about you being ambushed in there." He cleared his throat. "I'm sorry I didn't tell you I was considering reenlisting."

"You don't owe me anything, Jesse. I understand, and I don't regret any part of this past week." Her voice shook and she stiffened her back. "I learned some things from you that I will always be grateful for."

"I wasn't hiding the reenlistment from you," he said. "From my family, yes. I purposefully kept them in the dark."

She still wouldn't look at him, but the rhythm of her strokes changed. Her hand slowed until Caleb lowered his head and nudged her with his muzzle to continue.

"The end of the year was my deadline. I wasn't going to tell them until after I made the decision. They would've tried to change my mind and I wanted to stay as objective as possible. What a farce. I know that now, because of you."

She lowered her hand and turned to look at him. Her face was pale, her eyes shadowed. She didn't speak.

"I'm not cut out for the military. I joined partly because it was expected, but also because I was feeling restless and displaced. When I was given the opportunity to learn to fly I thought maybe a military career was the answer." He sighed. "Then I got homesick. I hoped I'd come back to the Sundance and things would be different. If I learned to fly a chopper I could help bring the place into the twenty-first century. Roundup would be a breeze, we could expand… The truth is, I wanted to come back and be a hero. I wanted to be needed. I wanted to feel as if I belonged here again."

Shivering, she hugged herself and rubbed her arms.

He wanted to hold her. It would be so easy to justify pulling her close. "You were totally right the other night. My family never made me feel those things. They've never stopped loving me or had a single thought that I didn't deserve a place here. The economy doesn't matter. We could be down to our last dollar and I would be no more dispensable than Cole or Trace or Rachel. I'm a McAllister. They didn't forget that. I did."

He almost choked on that admission and had to look away for a moment. "The thing is, I didn't get all that until—I don't know, maybe it all finally came together today. But the truth is, I didn't tell you about reenlisting because it's been one of the furthest things from my mind. This past week, with you, I was happy—" He stopped to swallow. "I didn't believe I could ever be this happy again, and I didn't want the feeling to go away. I don't want it to go away."

He moved closer to her and she took a step toward him.

"I'd miss you, Shea. I'd miss your courage. I could handle being a soldier again if I had to, I could handle deployment. I can handle anything except not having you in my life. I love you." He took the last few steps to reach her but she was already flinging herself at him. He caught her in his arms. She'd taught him how to love and be loved. He had a feeling he had a lot more to learn from her.

"Oh, Jesse." She sniffed and buried her face against his neck. "My feet aren't touching the ground so don't drop me."

"Is that all you have to say?" He laughed, letting himself breathe now that he knew he hadn't blown the best thing to ever happen to him.

"I'm thinking."

"I'll save you some brain power," he said, and felt her smile against his skin. "It's only been a week, I know. But I've never been more sure of anything in my life." He kissed her ear, her hair. Loosening his hold, he let her slide down his body until her feet hit the floor and their eyes met. "I know you have a job you love in San Jose, but somehow we can make this work. If you want to."

A slow smile lifted her lips as if she had a secret no one else knew. "I do want to," she said. "I want you."

Jesse held her face between his hands and kissed her. Kissed her with everything he had. He wasn't much for talking, but he'd be damned if he wasn't going to show her that he meant every one of those three words.

Hearing her whimper made him feel like he could do anything. Right now that meant picking her up again and taking her straight over to the long ladder leading up to the loft.

"What are you doing?" she asked, her breathlessness making him grin.

"There are a few things a city slicker like you still doesn't know about life on a ranch."

"For example?"

He set her down, but they wouldn't be apart for long. "Like what a real roll in the hay is like."

"Hay?" she asked, her smile getting a little wobbly. "Scratchy hay?"

He laughed. What else was he going to do with a woman like Shea? "Trust me."

Caleb whinnied as they raced up the ladder, but the horse was out of luck. Shea was all his.

* * * * *

COMING NEXT MONTH FROM HARLEQUIN® BLAZE™

Available December 18, 2012

#729 THE RISK-TAKER • *Uniformly Hot!*
by Kira Sinclair

Returned POW Gage Harper is no hero, and the last thing he wants is to relive his story. But can he resist when Hope Rawlings, the girl he could never have, is willing to do anything to get it?

#730 LYING IN BED • *The Wrong Bed*
by Jo Leigh

Right bed...wrong woman. When FBI agent Ryan Vail goes undercover at a ritzy resort to investigate a financial scam at an intimacy retreat for couples, he'll have to call on all his skills. Like pretending to be in love with his "wife" aka fellow agent—and almost one-night stand—Angie Wolf.

#731 HIS KIND OF TROUBLE • *The Berringers*
by Samantha Hunter

Bodyguard Chance Berringer must tame the feisty celebrity chef Ana Perez to protect her. Only, the heat between them is unstoppable and so may be the danger....

#732 ONE MORE KISS by Katherine Garbera

When a whirlwind Vegas courtship goes bust, Alysse Dresden realizes she has to pick up the pieces and move on. Now, years later, her ex insists he'll win her back! Alysse is reluctant, yet she can't deny Jay Cutler is the one man she's never forgotten.

#733 RELENTLESS SEDUCTION by Jillian Burns

A girls' weekend in New Orleans sounded like the breakout event Claire Brooks has been waiting for. But when her friend goes missing, Claire admits she needs the help of local Rafe Moreau, a mysterious loner. Rafe's raw sensuality tempts Claire like no other...and she can't say no!

#734 THE WEDDING FLING by Meg Maguire

Tabloid-shy actress Leigh Bailey has always avoided scandal. But she's bound to make the front page when she escapes on a tropical honeymoon getaway—without her groom! Lucky her hunky pilot Will Burgess is there to make sure she doesn't get too lonely....

YOU CAN FIND MORE INFORMATION ON UPCOMING HARLEQUIN© TITLES, FREE EXCERPTS AND MORE AT WWW.HARLEQUIN.COM.

HBCNM1212

REQUEST YOUR FREE BOOKS!

2 FREE NOVELS PLUS 2 FREE GIFTS!

red-hot reads!

YES! Please send me 2 FREE Harlequin® Blaze™ novels and my 2 FREE gifts (gifts are worth about $10). After receiving them, if I don't wish to receive any more books, I can return the shipping statement marked "cancel." If I don't cancel, I will receive 6 brand-new novels every month and be billed just $4.49 per book in the U.S. or $4.96 per book in Canada. That's a saving of at least 14% off the cover price. It's quite a bargain. Shipping and handling is just 50¢ per book in the U.S. and 75¢ per book in Canada.* I understand that accepting the 2 free books and gifts places me under no obligation to buy anything. I can always return a shipment and cancel at any time. Even if I never buy another book, the two free books and gifts are mine to keep forever.

151/351 HDN FEQE

Name (PLEASE PRINT)

Address Apt. #

City State/Prov. Zip/Postal Code

Signature (if under 18, a parent or guardian must sign)

Mail to the **Reader Service:**

IN U.S.A.: P.O. Box 1867, Buffalo, NY 14240-1867

IN CANADA: P.O. Box 609, Fort Erie, Ontario L2A 5X3

Not valid for current subscribers to Harlequin Blaze books.

Want to try two free books from another line?
Call 1-800-873-8635 or visit www.ReaderService.com.

* Terms and prices subject to change without notice. Prices do not include applicable taxes. Sales tax applicable in N.Y. Canadian residents will be charged applicable taxes. Offer not valid in Quebec. This offer is limited to one order per household. All orders subject to credit approval. Credit or debit balances in a customer's account(s) may be offset by any other outstanding balance owed by or to the customer. Please allow 4 to 6 weeks for delivery. Offer available while quantities last.

Your Privacy—The Reader Service is committed to protecting your privacy. Our Privacy Policy is available online at www.ReaderService.com or upon request from the Reader Service.

We make a portion of our mailing list available to reputable third parties that offer products we believe may interest you. If you prefer that we not exchange your name with third parties, or if you wish to clarify or modify your communication preferences, please visit us at www.ReaderService.com/consumerschoice or write to us at Reader Service Preference Service, P.O. Box 9062, Buffalo, NY 14269. Include your complete name and address.

HB11B

SPECIAL EXCERPT FROM HARLEQUIN® BLAZE™

Bestselling Blaze author Jo Leigh delivers a sizzling *The Wrong Bed* story with

Lying in Bed

Ryan woke to the bed dipping. For a few seconds, his adrenaline spiked until he remembered where he was. He groaned at the bright red numbers on the clock. "One a.m.? What…?"

The rest of the question got lost in the dark, but it didn't matter, because Jeannie didn't answer. His fellow agent on this sting must be exhausted after arriving late. "You okay?"

She tugged sharply on the covers, pulling more of them to her side of the bed.

Ryan could just make out her head on the pillow, her back to him, hunched and tight. Must have gotten stuck at the airport….

He curled onto his side, hoping to find the dream she'd interrupted. It had been nice. Smelled nice. He sighed as he let himself slip deeper and deeper into sleep…. The scent came back, a little like the beach and jasmine, low-key and sexy—

His eyes flew open. His heart thudded as his pulse raced. No need to panic. That was Jeannie next to him. Who else would it be?

Undercover jitters. It happened. Not to him, but he'd heard tales. Moving slowly, Ryan twisted until he could see his bed partner.

He swallowed as his gaze went to the back of Jeannie's head. Was it the moonlight? Jeannie's blond hair looked darker. And longer. He moved closer, took a deep breath.

"What the—" Ryan sat up so fast the whole bed shook. His hand flailed in his search for the light switch.

It wasn't Jeannie next to him. Jeannie smelled like baby powder and bananas. The woman next to him smelled exactly like…

She groaned, and as she turned over, he whispered, "No, no, no, no."

Special Agent Angie Wolf glared back at him with red-rimmed eyes.

"Jeannie is being held over in court," she snapped. "I'd rather not be here, but we don't have much choice if we want to salvage the operation."

She punched the pillow, looked once more in his direction and said, "Oh, and if you wake me before eight, I'll kill you with my bare hands," then pulled the covers over her head.

No way could Ryan pretend to be married to Angie Wolf. This operation was possible because Jeannie and he were buddies. Hell, he was pals with her husband and played with her kids.

Angie Wolf was another story. She was hot, for one thing. Hot as in smokin' hot. Tall, curvy and those legs…

God, just a few hours ago, he'd been laughing about the Intimate at Last brochure. Body work. Couples massages. *Delightful homeplay assignments.* How was this supposed to work now?

Ryan stared into the darkness. Angie Wolf was going to be his wife. For a week. Holy hell.

Pick up LYING IN BED by Jo Leigh.
On sale December 18, 2012, from Harlequin Blaze.

Copyright © 2013 by Jolie Kramer

HBEXP1212JLREV

She sat clutching the wheel with sweaty hands, her heart pounding, poised to flee like a bird. She did not want to face this. Not tonight, not when Ryan's reentry into her life had shaken her up so much.

But then a dark figure loomed up next to her van, and it was too late to flee.

She lowered her window slowly. Ryan leaned down, his handsome face speckled with snowflakes, and smiled at her. "I'm glad you came," he said softly.

"You wretch," she retorted. "You didn't tell me there would be anyone else."

"They're leaving in a short while," he told her. "In any case, you know them both, Penny. And they're dying to see you. Switch off your engine and come in."

An English-literature graduate, **MADELEINE KER** has been writing for over two decades. Her first Harlequin romance novel was titled *Aquamarine,* and was published in 1983. Since then, she has penned thirty-three novels for Harlequin as well as a number of thrillers. She describes herself as "a compulsive writer," and is very excited by the way women's fiction is evolving. She is also a compulsive traveler and has lived in many different parts of the world, including Britain, Italy, Spain and South Africa. She has a young family (whom she has "relentlessly dragged around the world") and a number of pets.